THE FLIGHT OF PETO'S KEY

MATTHEW BERGER

DEDICATION

To Northern Michigan – the place I love, hate and occasionally curse under my breath. I've seen you in your glory and in your grit, in sunshine that makes the world stand still and winters that make you question why anyone lives here at all. When you are at your best, there's no better place to be. When you're not…well, you're still home.

TABLE OF CONTENTS

INTRODUCTION
THE MISSION

They came typed on thin carbon paper, the ink already fading before the crews ever touched the cockpit. To headquarters they were lines of instruction; to the men, they were maps of survival—ink that would turn into cloud and ice, hunger and silence, the roar of engines, and the thought of a home that waited far beyond the mountains.

CONFIDENTIAL
   Operational Orders – 1327th AAF Base Unit
   Assam–China Ferry Route ("The Hump")

HEADQUARTERS
   10th AIR FORCE

APO 465, U.S. Army
22 MAY 1944

FIELD ORDER NO. 117
(Extract)
SITUATION
a. Allied supply requirements in China re-
main critical to support operations of the
Chinese Army and U.S. Air Units operat-
ing under the Fourteenth Air Force.
b. Weather reports indicate monsoon activ-
ity increasing along the Assam–Burma–
China route. Expect turbulence, icing,
and heavy cloud cover above 12,000 feet.
Enemy fighter presence remains minimal
but not discounted.

MISSION
The following crews of the 1327th Army
Air Force Base Unit will conduct aerial resupply
operations ("Hump" transport) from Chabua,
Assam, India to Kunming, China. Aircraft: C-47
Skytrain. Cargo: medical supplies, spare parts,

and high-octane aviation fuel. Delivery is to be completed no later than 23 MAY 1944.

EXECUTION
    a. Primary Route: Depart Chabua 0600 hours. Climb to 14,000 feet crossing Patkai Range. Proceed direct over Fort Hertz and onward across the Salween River to Kunming.
    b. Alternate Route: Via Ledo–Myitkyina–Yunnan corridor. Adjust altitude per weather.
    c. Radio silence to be maintained except in emergency.
    d. Cargo to remain secured under direction of Loadmaster. Engineer to inspect tie-downs prior to departure.

ADMINISTRATION & LOGISTICS
    a. Fuel and rations issued at Chabua.
    b. Crew survival kits to be carried per regulation. Jungle and mountain conditions anticipated in event of forced landing.

COMMAND & SIGNAL
 a. Aircraft Commander: Capt. J. Whitaker.
 b. Radio call sign: "Dogtail Four."
 c. Challenge and reply per code sheet No. 73.
 d. Report mission completion to Operations, 1327th AAFBU, immediately upon return.

BY ORDER OF BRIGADIER GENERAL TUNNER
/s/
R.E. HARKINS
Major, Air Corps
Operations Officer

The orders ended there. Plain words on paper. But for the men who carried them, those lines would soon take the shape of mountains and storms, the weight of silence above the clouds, and the quiet thought of home—whatever corner of the world that meant—held close as they flew into the dark.

CHAPTER ONE
THE NAME ON THE NOSE

Captain Jack Whitaker stood beneath the wing of the battered C-47, eyeing the storm clouds coiling above the Burmese jungle. His leather jacket was soaked through at the shoulders.

The crew was gathering – Murphy and La-Clair, once gunners and now loadmasters; Sayers, the ever-steady mechanic and young Tommy Dillard, the radio operator who still carried his baseball mitt in his duffel, like it might bring stateside a little closer.

Broad-shouldered and quiet as a thunderstorm, Murphy always had an unlit cigarette tucked behind one ear and a scowl that could send a sergeant packing.

LeClair wore his grin like armor, Louisiana

drawl thick as molasses as he greeted the ground crew like old poker buddies. He had a habit of tapping the plane's nose three times before boarding, like it owed him a favor.

Sayers kept to himself, grease under his fingernails and a photo of his twin daughters folded neat in his shirt pocket. He talked to the engines like they understood him.

Tommy always showed up five minutes early, hovering like he was waiting for permission to belong. His voice had a habit of cracking, but once he was behind the radio, it turned to steel.

Jack watched them for a moment, knowing every quirk, every habit. These men were as familiar to him as the sound of the engines, and just as vital to getting home in one piece.

"Load her up tight and tie her down twice. Wheels up at oh-five hundred," Jack barked, glancing at the large white block letters painted across the nose of his plane: PETO'S KEY.

"Damn painter can't spell," he muttered. Was supposed to read PETOSKEY—the way he'd written it carefully on the request sheet in his best captain's script. It wasn't just a name. It was home. Petoskey, Michigan—summer sunsets bleeding gold over Lake Michigan, winters when the shoreline froze solid and the wind cut like a knife. A place where the sky met the trees in postcard perfection. And Sarah—God, Sarah—on the porch on Howard Street, that little wave of hers catching the light, making him feel like the luckiest man alive. Not some damn tourist-trap beach town where people went to get sunburned.

Jack kept staring at the letters, the misspelling somehow sticking like a burr.

Tommy offered to repaint it, but LeClair swore it was bad luck to change a name once it was on the nose. Murphy said it was like carving a typo into a tombstone. Jack figured maybe Peto knew something they didn't. From then on, Peto's Key wasn't just a plane, it was a running joke, a lucky charm, and a promise. The crew swore Peto was their guardian spirit, riding shotgun on every haul across the Hump. And whenever the engines rattled or the wings iced over, LeClair would slap the wall and call out, "Still counting on you, Peto!"

Jack had been a foreman at the Michigan

Maple Block Company before trading lumber and late shifts for khakis and cockpit gauges. By twenty-four, he was used to the smell of sawdust and sweat, ruling the floor with quiet authority. He knew every machine by the sound it made and every man by the stories they never told. When the war started, he could have stayed— "essential industry," the papers called it. But that week, he watched his youngest brother, jaw clenched against fear, in a pressed uniform, step forward and hug their mother goodbye at the train depot. That was all the push he needed. A month later, he enlisted in the Air Corps.

That was months ago. Now he stood half a world away, on a strip of mud and steel framed by jungle and mountains.

The sun hadn't risen yet, but the airfield already steamed with heat, engine grease, and nerves. Flying "The Hump"—the aerial supply route over the eastern Himalayas—was anything but simple. It was the kind of country God must have made when he was in a in a lousy mood.

Pilots flew into sudden storms that slammed the wings sideways, hurricane-force winds clawing at the fuselage. Turbulence could drop a plane thousands of feet in the time it took to curse. Ice crept across the wings, engines coughed and froze, and the world outside the windshield could vanish in a blink. Japanese fighters prowled the skies, and while the mountains might hide you for a heartbeat, their knife-edge ridges left nowhere to turn. The planes were overloaded, patched together, and all too willing to quit at altitude. If you went down, no one was coming quickly, the mountains were too high, the jungle too thick, and the weather could turn any rescue into a suicide run.

And this morning, every man on Peto's Key knew it.

Inside Peto's Key's corrugated shell, the air was thick with oil, sweat, and the scrape of boots on metal. The crew moved with the urgency of veterans and the rhythm of a bar fight. Sayers hauled a wooden crate of .50-caliber belts up the aluminum belly. Nearby, LeClair handled the most sacred cargo, a small tin box of letters from home, slipped carefully into his parachute satchel. Murphy crouched by the tie-downs, checking each crate latch with two hard tugs before nodding to no one in particular. He lit a Camel, took a slow drag, and said, "Tell me again why we're the delivery boys instead of the damn post office."

LeClair didn't even look up. "Because the post office doesn't fly over the damn Himalayas—and neither would you if you had any sense."

Murphy smirked. "Good thing sense isn't in the job description."

As Jack reviewed the flight manifest near the nose of Peto's Key, a young staff sergeant strode up with a duffel in one hand and a cocky grin that reeked of too many close calls.

"Orders say I'm hitching a ride to Kunming," the kid said. "Ed Klines. But most folks call me Lucky."

Jack didn't take his hand. He just gave him a long once-over—mud-spattered boots, jacket too clean, and a silver Saint Christopher medal swinging from one strap.

"They call you what now?"

"Lucky," the sergeant repeated, grin holding.

"It's a joke, mostly. I've walked away from two crash landings, a munitions depot fire, and dysentery. Kind of stuck."

Jack drew a slow breath through his nose, letting it out like steam from a kettle just before it screams.

"I got two rules in this war, Klines," he said, tapping the clipboard with his pencil. "First—if you've got a bad feeling about a mission, you don't go. Doesn't matter what the brass says."

The kid started to speak, but Jack cut him off with a raised finger. "Second—you don't share a foxhole or a cockpit with anyone called Lucky. Their streak's about to end or worse, yours is. And when the bill comes due, it always gets paid in blood."

Jack drew a line through the name on his clipboard. "Catch the next C-109. Fuel run leaves at noon. Tell them I sent you."

Klines hesitated. "Isn't that a tanker? I heard they rattle like coffee cans."

"They do," Jack said. "But they don't carry me."

The kid walked off slower, grin fading. From

the wing, LeClair chuckled. "You always this jumpy about names, Cap? Or is this just your Lucky charm rule?"

Jack glanced after Klines, then back at his clipboard. "Nah. Just old enough to respect the odds."

LeClair shook his head, still grinning. "Remind me never to play cards with you."

Jack didn't linger. The day was moving, and so were they.

Jack climbed the short steps into Peto's Key, the metal skin warm under his gloves. He didn't like leaving anyone behind, but superstition had sharper teeth than reason at altitude.

At the top of the ramp, he glanced over his shoulder. Lucky Klines still stood at the edge of the field, one hand shading his eyes against the sun, the other raised in what could have been a hesitant farewell—or a quiet blessing. Jack nodded once, more to himself than to the man below, then stepped inside.

The cabin buzzed with motion. Sayers finished buttoning the access panel near the right throttle assembly, giving Jack a thumbs-up before dropping into his seat with the resignation of a man who could read an engine by its heartbeat. Murphy was lashing the last crate into place with military precision. LeClair checked the door rigging, cigarette dangling from his mouth and a low hymn humming out between his teeth. Tommy sat at the comms console already strapped in, fingers drumming against his knees, the baseball mitt resting in his lap. He looked up as Jack passed, goggles pushed high on his forehead.

Jack gave him a nod and slid into the left seat. The leather cushion was cracked in all the familiar places. The control yoke felt like an old friend—one you trusted even when you didn't trust the world.

"Alright," he said into the intercom, flipping a row of switches above his head. "Let's keep her in one piece today."

"Copy that," LeClair replied, a grin audible in his voice. "Let's go see if the sky forgot how to kill us."

Jack adjusted the flaps, checked the fuel pressure gauges—everything in the green—then shoved the throttles forward. The engines came alive with a guttural roar, vibrating through the frame. Peto's Key surged ahead, her wheels biting into the dirt strip as prop wash tore at the grass and peppered the fuselage with grit.

The acceleration pressed Jack back into his seat. The jungle blurred on both sides, a green smear in his periphery. The tail lifted, the nose strained upward. Airspeed climbed. "V one," he called. No one answered—they didn't need to.

He eased back on the yoke. The wheels broke free, the ground dropping away in a rush of silence and weightlessness. Behind him, LeClair gave the bulkhead three sharp knocks. "Let's climb, Peto. Don't let us down."

At the edge of the runway, boots planted in red clay, Ed "Lucky" Klines watched the plane bank west into the rising wind, the name on her nose catching the sun: PETO'S KEY—a typo turned totem. The C-47 dwindled into the haze over the jungle. His lips moved, words lost to the prop wash: "Fly safe, boys. Hope that bucket has one more run in her."

CHAPTER TWO
GOD'S ATTIC

The altimeter spun higher as Peto's Key surged westward and slipped into the slate-gray mist. Below, the jagged ridges of the Himalayas disappeared beneath a roiling sea of cloud—endless, soundless, like a world holding its breath.

Captain Jack Whitaker scanned the sky through frost-dusted glass, adjusting the trim to compensate for the wind clawing at the fuselage. The intercom crackled.

"Got movement. Three o'clock, low!" LeClair's voice crackled through the intercom, sharp and tense.

Jack snapped his head toward the starboard side just as a tear in the cloud cover revealed the silhouette of three shapes. Japanese Ki-43

Oscars—sleek, single-engine fighters with long, elegant wings—cut through the mist in tight formation, their camouflage of mottled green and brown flickering like ghosts in the clouds. Fast, nimble, and unforgiving, their engine growl rose from below like distant thunder sharpening its teeth.

"Damn it!" Jack's voice was sharp, guttural, his hands already working the controls. "Tighten up and stay steady—we so much as flinch, those bastards will be on us like rust on rivets."

"They see us?" Murphy growled, his voice low and dangerous.

"Unless that's a new kind of Japanese greeting, I don't think they're waving," LeClair shot back, already sliding into the waist gun position.

Jack's mind raced. Peto's Key could not outrun fighters—she was not built for that. But she might outfly them through the only thing she had on her side: weather.

"Strap in, gentlemen," he said into the intercom, his voice tight with command. "We're going up."

He pitched the nose sharply and climbed toward the upper shelf of clouds. Thunderheads swelled like stone spires in every direction, their jagged peaks hiding the sky beyond. Moisture clung to the windows, feathering into ice.

Tommy glanced at the frost building along the radio console. "Cap… we're icing."

"I see it," Jack said, his voice steady but edged with tension. "Sayers, I need temps and engine response every sixty seconds."

"Already on it," the mechanic called back, his tone low but unwavering.

The wings of Peto's Key shimmered with a dangerous sheen, and the engines began to labor, coughing against the thinning air. The patrol behind them grew smaller in the rearview but not gone—still too close.

"That's too much ice, Cap," Murphy said. "We're flying a goddamn popsicle."

Jack adjusted altitude again, trying to thread the line between death by bullets and death by stall. The plane lurched. The altimeter needle jittered.

"She's still got lift," Jack said, more to himself than anyone. "Come on, old girl. Just a little higher."

Behind him, LeClair let out a breath. "I don't think they followed."

"Course not," Jack said, his gaze flicking back over his shoulder one last time. "They're smart enough to stay out of God's attic when He's not home."

Jack exhaled. Still, the tension gnawed at him. He muttered into the mic, "Stay sharp. They're gone, but the sky's not done with us."

Then came the shudder.

It started as a flutter under the yoke, then turned into a full-body lurch that rocked the fuselage. Jack gripped the controls as the C-47 pitched slightly to port. Through the frosting glass, he could see the problem: the wings, feathered in ice, were losing lift. Fast.

"Temps just dropped again," Sayers called from the bulkhead, his voice tight with focus. "Starboard aileron's not responding clean. She's icing deep, Cap."

Frost spidered across the glass, and the right engine wheezed as ice pulled at the prop blades.

"The wings are icing up and we're running out of sky," Jack growled, his hands working the controls with urgency. "Clear that anti-ice line or pick a tree to crash into."

Tommy was already unbuckling from the comms bench. "If it's just blocked, I can clear it."

Murphy looked at him like he'd grown a second head. "You're not going out there. You even know what you're looking for?"

"Line runs just under the wing root," Tommy said, pulling on his gloves with determination. "Carries heated fluid—keeps ice from forming on the leading edge. I saw Sayers flush one on the ground last week."

"Yeah, well, this ain't the ground," Murphy muttered, eyes narrowing.

Jack twisted in his seat, his gaze sharp. "Tommy—"

"I'm the smallest," Tommy said simply, without hesitation. "I can get out onto the wing root, check the nozzle housing. If it's just a block or a split line, I can vent it."

There wasn't time to debate. The yoke vibrated in Jack's hand like a living nerve, and the plane was dipping, sagging with slow inevitability. Altitude bleeding away by the second.

Jack hesitated, the weight of the decision pressing down on him. Every part of him screamed to stop the kid, but the seconds were ticking away, and there was no other choice. The weight of responsibility pressed down on him like the entire mountain range. "If you're sure you can reach it and you don't die trying—go. We've got maybe sixty seconds of lift left."

LeClair growled under his breath. "I swear, if that kid dies, I'm gonna haunt this damn plane."

Tommy was already cinching the safety harness attached to the bulkhead around his waist.

Jack met his eyes, voice hard with command. "You get out there, you clear it, and you get back. You fall, I'm turning this crate around and crashing it just to come find you."

Tommy grinned—just a flash of nerves and grit. "Understood, sir."

LeClair clipped the rope into Tommy's harness and slapped his shoulder. "Go earn your wings, kid."

The access hatch opened, and the roar outside punched through the fuselage, a storm unleashed. Tommy crawled onto the narrow maintenance catwalk, the wind clawing at him like an unseen predator. Frost laced every surface like the jungle had been dipped in crystal.

He reached the housing above the starboard wing. His gloves slipped once—he steadied himself with a knee hooked over the fuselage rail, breath fogging the air like steam from a kettle.

He popped the release valve. Nothing.

Then—crack. A shard of ice broke loose. The nozzle hissed. Fluid sprayed.

From the cockpit, Jack felt the sluggish aileron twitch back to life.

"She's responding," Sayers called from the bulkhead, voice tinged with hope. "Lift's coming back."

"Tommy?" Jack said into the intercom, voice tight with focus.

Static. Then— "Climbing back in. I missed my chance to die by ten seconds. Sorry to disappoint, LeClair."

The crew laughed—short, nervous bursts, the tension finally breaking. Jack smiled, just for a moment, the weight lifting from his chest.

But the victory was brief.

Warning lights flared on the dash. Engine two was coughing, pressure dropping.

Jack's jaw tightened, his eyes scanning the gauges. "Sayers, we're losing power. What's she saying?"

"She's saying we're landing," Sayers called back, his voice steady but laced with concern. "Engine two's iced too deep. We're out of sky."

Jack adjusted the flaps, his gaze darting to the jungle canopy below. A clearing or the shadow of one—maybe five hundred yards across.

"Brace for landing," he ordered, voice hard and commanding. "Strap in and pray to Peto."

The jungle rose up like a fist.

Jack fought the yoke, fighting against the pull of the dying engine as the clearing rushed toward them—less a runway, more a rough patch of tall grass and panic, ringed in towering hardwoods and strangler figs. He dropped the flaps, coaxing the last bit of lift from the starboard engine, praying it would hold just a little longer.

Peto's Key slammed into the clearing with a shriek of metal and torn earth. The rear skids caught hard, bouncing them once before the front gear folded with a sickening crunch. Crates snapped their restraints. The fuselage groaned— groaned again, pitching sideways. Branches exploded against the wings, splintering. Something important sheared off behind the cockpit, a loud, metallic scream. The plane listed sideways, groaning like it was dying in stages. The sound of snapping branches gave way to dead quiet—and then the sharp, wet drip of coolant.

Jack's head throbbed. His collar was damp— smoke, sweat, or blood—he wasn't sure. His breath came heavy as he unbuckled with a grunt and turned to check on the crew.

"Sound off," he croaked, his voice thick with grit.

"Still here," Sayers muttered from behind, rubbing his shoulder with a grimace.

"Murphy," came a grunt. "Bruised, not broken."

"LeClair?" Jack called again, heart pounding.

A coughing laugh. "She flies like hell, but she crashes smooth."

That left— "Tommy?"

Silence.

Tommy blinked up at the ceiling, lips cracked, trying to flex his fingers before realizing he couldn't feel them at all.

"Tommy!" Jack twisted out of his seat, stumbling aft.

He found him slumped near the comms bench, wrapped in the shredded flight harness. The kid was pale, shivering, his fingers already blotched with purple and white.

Jack swore under his breath. "We need heat. Now. And a signal."

The crew moved like wounded wolves. LeClair scavenged for their emergency thermal blankets. Murphy hacked through mangled crates to find rations and dry canvas. Sayers checked Tommy's hands and face. "This is a damn joke," he muttered, his voice thick with disbelief. "We're boiling in a jungle, and he's got frostbite."

Sayers nodded grimly, gently unwrapping the kid's hands. The fingertips were ghostly white, edges already turning waxy with the early burn of exposure. "He got iced bad," the mechanic murmured. "Wing walk at altitude, bare minutes of exposure—but up there, that's all it takes."

Murphy cursed under his breath, then shoved aside a splintered crate. "So he freezes five miles up, and crashes sweating into a rainforest. Hell of a delivery route we signed up for."

Jack didn't laugh. He stood at the edge of the cargo bay, scanning the tree line as the last light drained from the canopy. When he spoke, his voice was low, flat, and almost lost in the hum of the jungle.

"That's the Hump," he said. "You freeze on the way in, you burn on the way out. Sky's full of riddles, ground's full of snakes. Everything in between is trying to kill you."

He turned back to Tommy, who was trying—and failing—not to cry out as Sayers wrapped his hands in gauze.

They rigged a signal post using the busted aerial from the cockpit, mounted onto a tree with broken cargo straps. LeClair cobbled together a makeshift power supply from battery leads and the auxiliary nav light system—his hands shaking from adrenaline and blood loss from a gash along his calf.

By nightfall, the jungle buzzed and growled. Cicadas screamed like warning sirens. Somewhere distant, something howled.

Inside the wreckage, the radio crackled weakly to life.

Tommy, wrapped in blankets and shame, whispered through chattering teeth, "I'll take the first shift."

Jack shook his head, his voice rough with weariness. "You've done enough for one day, kid."

But the boy's eyes were defiant through the pain. "No radio, no rescue. I can twist a dial with two fingers, can't I?"

Jack relented with a sigh. He placed a hand on Tommy's shoulder, then joined LeClair and Murphy outside, where the canopy arched overhead like a cathedral built by vines.

They took turns through the night, passing the headset like a communion chalice. No replies came. Only static. But they kept at it.

Because the only thing worse than falling out of the sky… was falling and being forgotten.

CHAPTER THREE
THE SMOKE AND THE SIGNAL

By the time night swallowed the crash site, the jungle had already begun to reclaim the wreck. The crew, broken and battered, barely held onto what was left of their plane, their bodies worn from the crash and the heat of survival. The air was thick with moisture, and the vines were already creeping across the fuselage, as if the earth itself wanted the plane to disappear.

The jungle didn't sleep.

Cicadas pulsed in waves, rising and falling like distant artillery, a constant hum that rattled the edges of sanity. Somewhere beyond the broken plane, monkeys screamed—sharp, guttural cries that echoed like lost souls across the canopy. Every leaf was slick with dew, each drop clinging like a burden. Every breath came with the taste of wet moss, the sharp tang of rot, and something darker in the air—a scent of death too close to be ignored.

The crew of Peto's Key camped beneath the half-crumpled wing, a tarp stretched between mangled struts, glowing faintly orange from the pulsing flame of their ration-tin fire. The flickering light barely touched the darkness around them, casting long, twisted shadows. Nobody spoke unless they had to. The air felt too heavy for words.

Murphy kept watch, the borrowed flare gun resting across his knee like a silent promise, ready but waiting. LeClair had used a shard of mirror to stitch his calf, his face twisted in pain as he muttered through gritted teeth, the words lost beneath the pressure of each breath. Sayers worked quietly beside Tommy, his hands delicate as he wrapped the kid's fingers in gauze, tucking them beneath his armpits like precious cargo, his focus unwavering.

Jack hadn't slept. He sat at the edge of the tarp, radio in his lap, his fingers absently tracing the cold metal as he scanned the static wash for a signal. His face was unreadable, a mask of exhaustion and resolve. But his mind was elsewhere, unwilling to accept the quiet certainty that no rescue was coming. His eyes were locked on the dark, staring into the trees as if willing a signal to break through the static.

Sometime after midnight, the fire sputtered low, its glow faltering like the last breath of a dying thing. The radio crackled once more, wheezing its final string of static before sinking into a silent void. No contact. No carrier wave. Just the jungle. Its quiet was a weighty presence that pressed in from all sides, as if the earth itself was listening, and deciding not to hear.

The moon hung in pieces through the leaves, fragmented silver bleeding into black. It was as if the sky had forgotten how to shine.

A branch cracked nearby. Something moved.

Not far from the tree line, two yellow eyes blinked—low to the ground, unmoving. Then a low, rattling growl rumbled beneath the canopy.

"Eyes," Jack whispered, his voice barely a breath.

Murphy swung the flare gun around, finger resting but not pressing the trigger. LeClair, half-asleep, muttered, "That better not be one of those jungle leopards. I'm in no mood to be a midnight snack."

The eyes disappeared.

Then came the rustle of paws in the underbrush—growing louder, deliberate, like a predator closing in.

"Must've smelled the blood," Sayers said, not looking up from the smoldering fire. "Didn't like what it found."

The air tightened after that, a stillness thick as oil. Every man stayed close. No more jokes. Just breathing. Listening.

Jack sat beside Tommy in the faint orange glow of their sputtering fire tin, the jungle pressing in close on all sides. The humidity clung to them like gauze, sticky and suffocating, but Tommy still shivered under the thermal blanket, his frostbitten hands tucked close to his chest.

"You ever miss home?" Tommy asked, voice thin and raw. His gaze didn't leave the dark jungle beyond the wing.

Jack didn't answer right away. He traced a rivet line along the edge of the torn fuselage. "Every damn day."

"I live over on Woodland and State," Tommy offered after a pause. "My mom runs the post office window."

Jack turned his head slightly, his eyes softening. "I know that corner. Used to walk past it every Friday after the shift at the block company. Stopped for coffee at that little shop that burned down in '40."

Tommy smiled faintly, the memory bittersweet. "My sister worked there."

Jack huffed out a laugh. "Hell of a small town, isn't it?" He paused, his voice low. "Petoskey... never thought I'd be so damn far from it."

For a moment, the jungle noise softened beneath the weight of their shared memory. Jack leaned back, his eyes tracing the patchy canopy above.

"There's this hill out past Mitchell Street—clears out just enough in winter that you can see all the way to the waterfront and the Midway. After the snow settles, everything turns this pale blue, like the town's holding its breath. Cold enough to bite your nose, but still quiet. Like the whole place knows you by name."

Tommy nodded slowly, the weight of nostalgia in his voice. "I used to walk there after school, throw rocks out on the ice until spring broke it."

They sat in silence, miles away from snowbanks and frozen sidewalks, until Tommy whispered, "Do you think we'll make it back?"

Jack didn't look at him. He stared into the shadows of the jungle, his voice quiet but firm. "We fell five miles out of the sky and landed with breath still in our lungs. That's got to count for something. Doesn't it?"

The last word lingered, heavy with an uncertainty he hadn't wanted to admit to himself.

Sayers, quiet until now, spoke from the shadows, his words low and steady. "Doesn't matter how far you fall. Home doesn't vanish. It just waits. Hard to believe a place like that still exists. Feels like we crashed on another planet."

All eyes turned to the broken silhouette of the plane.

"That's why you named the plane, isn't it?" LeClair's voice cut through the silence, soft but knowing.

Jack nodded. "Not what the painter got, but yeah. That's what I wrote on the requisition sheet. PETOSKEY. Figured if I named her right, she might remember where to take me."

Tommy smiled faintly, cradling his hands close, the warmth of the moment a fragile thing. "Even with frostbite, the jungle doesn't smell half as bad when you think about home."

A moment later, from somewhere far off—a mechanical thump. Faint. Then silence.

Jack stiffened, his body rigid, every muscle locked. His breath caught—just once, sharp and sudden. No thunder. No wind. Just that rhythm— one his bones knew all too well.

Engines. Unmistakable. They sliced through the jungle like a blade through fog. For a heart-beat, Jack wasn't sure if it was real. But then the tension slammed into him, and the fire flickered, dancing in sync with the pounding of his pulse.

Then again closer.

Jack didn't move, didn't speak, just

listened. His breath caught in his throat, each second stretching like a wire pulled taut. His pulse quickened, the silence amplifying every sound in the jungle. The others turned slowly toward the trees.

Then—there it was. A pulse. Dull, rhythmic. The unmistakable thump of an engine echoing off the hills. Distant, but real.

Jack stood. "Gear up. That is a bird looking for someone."

"Looking for us," LeClair said, already slinging on his pack.

Sayers hauled the flare bundle from its tin with practiced haste. Murphy raised the launcher, eyes narrowed, already in sync with the movement.

"Let's light it up," Jack said. "Give 'em a story to follow."

The flare hissed through the jungle canopy, red and righteous, carving a line through the night like a second sunrise. The men stared skyward—eyes wide, hearts pounding. Hope, in a thin line of fire.

"Here's hoping someone's awake on the

other end," muttered LeClair, the words a mix of hope and wariness.

The flare had barely burned out before the jungle came alive. For a moment, there was nothing but the crackling of leaves in the dying glow. Then, another sound cut through the night—soft, rhythmic, deliberate.

Bootsteps.

Coming fast.

Sayers crouched low and tapped Jack's boot. "Two groups. One's local—light-footed, closing fast from the west. But the others…" He looked up, mouth tight, his brow furrowing in unease. "Metal. Leather. Too clean."

Jack nodded grimly. "Japanese patrol. They're not just passing through."

LeClair cursed under his breath, reaching for the last rifle—Murphy's bolt-action with five rounds and no backup. "We are throwing rocks after this?"

"Let's hope it doesn't come to that," Jack muttered.

Tommy stirred beneath his blankets, fevered but awake. "Is it us they're after?"

Murphy grunted. "We dropped a flare like a damn invitation. They're coming for someone. It might as well be us."

Jack weighed the sounds—the cadence of trained boots against the lighter tread of bare feet on root. The two groups were closing in, fast. Their footsteps grew louder, a drumbeat in the thick air.

Then, from the west, a whistle. Not military. It thrilled like a bird, but in the stillness of the jungle, it sounded wrong, like a warning. The trill broke into three sharp, staccato chirps.

Sayers exhaled, his shoulders sagging slightly in relief, but his eyes remained alert. "Locals."

LeClair leaned out from behind a broken prop blade, eyes narrowing. "And they brought friends."

Out from the undergrowth spilled half a dozen villagers—mud-camouflaged, silent, armed with machetes and old Lee-Enfield rifles. The lead scout motioned sharply: Come.

Jack didn't hesitate. "Move! Grab what you can!"

Sayers lifted Tommy gently, one arm under

his shoulders, his movements swift but careful. Murphy and LeClair grabbed packs and slung what was left of the radio between them. Jack brought up the rear, scanning the jungle as they retreated.

They were moving before the sound of the boots grew louder—now unmistakable. The sharp rhythm of heavy footsteps, echoing off the trees. Voices in clipped Japanese. A barked order.

The rescue team led them along a narrow trail barely wider than a rifle barrel, snaking through dense ferns and vines. One villager dropped back, slipping into the brush. Moments later, a crack rang out—gunfire. Sharp and sudden, like a slap to the face. A warning, or maybe something more final.

They ran harder, feet pounding against the earth.

Jack glanced back once, just enough to catch sight of a plume of dark smoke rising above the trees, the flare's tail fading into vapor.

"They'll find the wreck," LeClair growled, his voice low but steady. "Let 'em. They'll be too late."

Thirty minutes later, breathless and soaked with sweat, they reached a stony slope hidden beneath a thicket of palms. An old British signal shack—abandoned but not forgotten. Half-swallowed by roots but still blinking with life.

The local leader handed Jack a folded note scrawled in Hindi and pidgin English. Jack tucked it into his shirt and turned to their unexpected saviors. "Thank you," he said, his voice raw, every word a struggle.

The man nodded once, then vanished into the green.

They hiked through darkness until the stars began to fade. When they reached the signal shack, the sun was already clawing through the mist. Then, they waited.

Four days they waited.

There was no firewood left, and the last of the rations had been scraped clean. Murphy joked that they were running on coffee grounds and prayer, but even he wasn't laughing by the second night. Jack rationed out melted snow in dented canteens, checking on Tommy every few hours. Frostbite was eating at his hands, turning them an angry shade of purple. Tommy grimaced each time Jack touched them but didn't say a word. LeClair's ankle had gone a worrying shade of plum. The rest of them were cold, hungry, and staring at the tree line like it owed them something.

On the fifth day, the jungle moved.

Not birds. Not wind. Men.

Dark shapes emerged from the underbrush—barefoot, lean, rifles slung across their shoulders, eyes sharp. Kachin. The same resistance fighters Jack had only heard about in briefings back in Assam. Behind them came two Americans in patched uniforms, one with an OSS armband and a Thompson cradled like a sleeping child.

"Captain Whitaker?" one of them asked, his accent clipped and Eastern. Boston, maybe.

Jack stood slowly, boots caked in red mud. "That's me."

The man grinned, a flash of teeth in the darkness. "Your bird's real damn lost. You're lucky these guys picked up your smoke. Strip's a week west. We march at first light."

"Medical?" Jack asked, eyes flicking to Tommy, whose hands were bundled in cloth and cradled against his chest.

"We've got morphine and a stretcher team," the man said, tossing Jack a battered canteen. "Hope your boys like rice and rats."

Murphy let out a weak laugh, the sound hoarse and dry in the cold air. "Better than snow and Spam."

The journey was brutal. River crossings that chilled to the bone. Leech-choked trails, the sting of cold-water seeping into their boots, and damp nights that seemed to drag on forever. But the Kachin moved like shadows, clearing paths with machetes, building fires that smoked just enough to keep the insects away but never enough to draw eyes from above.

One night, halfway to the strip, they camped in a narrow ravine. Jack sat beside LeClair near the embers of a small fire, both chewing on something pretending to be meat. Murphy snored nearby, his boots off and steaming.

"You think they'll scrap her?" LeClair asked, voice low.

Jack knew what he meant. "She's still up there. Holding together, maybe."

"Peto's Key deserves better than jungle rot."

"We all do."

LeClair nodded, his face shadowed in the firelight. "If they don't go back for her, I might. Someday. She's beat to hell, but she kept her promise."

Jack looked up at the stars—not that many were visible through the thick canopy. "You planning to live that long?"

"I plan to try."

A beat of silence passed between them.

Then Jack added, his voice quieter, "I left a toolbox under the navigator's bench. Still got Sarah's picture in it. If they pull her out, I want that back."

"Deal," LeClair said. "But you owe me a whiskey if I have to hike up there again."

Jack smiled, though it didn't reach his eyes. "You get her flying again; I'll buy the whole damn bottle."

When they finally reached the clearing, it wasn't much—just a pitted dirt strip and a few

British engineers smoking by the fuel drums. But there was a tent. And stretchers. And coffee. A C-47 stood ready with its engines warming, the sound comforting, almost like a promise. For the first time since the crash, Jack let himself believe it might be over.

He didn't look back at the jungle.

Because part of him already knew—Peto's Key wasn't done with them yet.

CHAPTER FOUR
THE SMELL OF CLEAN SHEETS

By the time they reached Myitkyina, the jungle was already a memory—still clinging to their boots, but fading beneath the smell of diesel, fresh canvas, and the faint metallic tang of the airstrip.

One moment, Jack was stepping off a battered jeep, the green still caked in his boot treads. The next, he was sitting in a British medical tent that smelled like bleach, cold coffee, sharp-cornered linens, and the low, steady hum of a generator. It didn't feel safe. Just a different kind of strange.

His new uniform hung loose on his frame—fatigues cinched with a parachute strap, boots polished by someone else. A clipboard hung at the foot of his cot. He hadn't read it. He didn't plan to.

Sayers slept across the aisle, snoring with one hand around a tin mug. LeClair was propped up nearby, his foot swaddled in rusted gauze, an unlit cigarette dangling from his lip like punctuation.

Murphy was, predictably, missing. Rumor had him holed up in a marathon poker game behind the latrines, holding court over a pile of British rations, two extra blankets, and a bottle of something the label insisted was medicinal.

Tommy had the worst of it, but you wouldn't know it by his mouth. In the main infirmary tent, hands swaddled in ice-soaked gauze, he sat upright cracking jokes. "Try taking a piss with lobster claws," he said to the nurse.

When she asked about the scorched baseball he clutched like an all-star shortstop, he told her: "My dad gave it to me. Said it brought better luck than saints." The ball had been in his flight jacket when they went down—a little scorched, but still there. When they cut the coat off him, he'd refused to let it go. She must've believed him—by the next morning, a battered glove had appeared on his cot. Left-handed, broken in, and exactly right. He slept with it beside him like it might catch dreams.

The debriefing had been just that—quick and brief. A desk-bound major with a voice like gravel ran through the motions: flight path, cargo weight, altitude, enemy contact, possible sabotage. Jack gave clipped, accurate answers. When it ended, the major muttered: "You're lucky, Captain. Most crews lost over the Hump stay lost."

Jack had replied, almost without meaning to: "We weren't waiting to be found. We were waiting to go home."

The words hung there, caught in the tent's filtered light. The major didn't respond.

After the debriefing, time stopped moving in straight lines. Mornings bled into chow, chow into cards, and somehow the sun kept rising. The jungle had let them go, but the quiet hadn't.

Tommy's hands were healing—red and tender, but intact. He drank orange concentrate from a tin can like it was scotch at the Petoskey Elks

Club. LeClair abandoned his crutches and resumed cursing anything that didn't work, which included the British laundry and their butchery of his last clean shirt.

Sayers found a jeep that wouldn't start and made it his mission to get back on the jungle path. "Wrench in hand, brain at peace," he said quietly to Jack one evening.

Murphy? He was thriving. By the third poker night, he'd cleaned out a half-dozen RAF gunners. His winnings included cigarettes, a tin of cocoa, and a pocketknife he named Eleanor. "The trick," he explained, shuffling with one hand, "is looking like you've got a winning hand, even if your cards are French and the game's mahjong."

LeClair piped up with a smirk, "Murphy once convinced a Red Cross nurse that he was the Duke of Essex. Got free morphine and a shoulder rub before anyone caught on."

"In my defense," Murphy said, deadpan, "I only said I could be the Duke. That ain't fraud. That's hope."

Jack laughed for the first time in days.

Word of the crew's survival had traveled fast.

A few mornings later, a runner summoned them to the field assembly tent. No one expected much—more paperwork or another round of temperature checks.

A general with shoulders like granite read from a clipboard.

"Captain Jack Whitaker," he said, "for exceptional airmanship under duress and the successful return of his crew: the Distinguished Flying Cross."

Jack stepped forward stiffly. The pin went just above his heart. He stared at the dirt the whole time.

The general's voice cut through the tent again: "Technician Thomas S. Darnell—for extraordinary bravery during emergency procedures and a mid-air wing walk under hostile conditions: the Silver Star."

Tommy blinked like he'd misheard. The applause was sharp, quick, and over too soon, like everyone was afraid to break the spell that had gotten them back. As the medal was pinned to his chest, he looked over at Jack, eyes wide, with a crooked grin.

"Guess we're really the Petoskey boys now," Tommy whispered.

Jack stepped forward, resting a hand on his shoulder. His voice was quiet but certain.

"Not a boy anymore, Tommy," he said. "You're a Petoskey man now."

Tommy didn't answer right away. He just nodded, blinking hard. The medal caught the light, but it was the look on his face that really shone.

That evening, with the weight of polished medals still fresh on their uniforms, they gathered around the same old crate as if it had never left. Cards, cocoa, cigarettes.

Murphy lost on purpose to a red-headed sergeant with a quartermaster brother. "That's not gambling," he explained. "That's investing."

LeClair leaned back, shaking his head. "He once mailed himself in a crate to skip KP. Claimed he was a box of replacement bolts."

"Worked, too," Murphy said. "Until some genius shipped me to Karachi."

The laughter came easy. Then quiet. Then still.

When Sayers finally said, "We owe you both," no one interrupted.

Tommy shrugged. "We had to get home. Jack just… pointed the way."

Outside, the clouds were low and pale. Jack finally opened Sarah's letter.

Her handwriting was neat, steady.

I heard about your crew. I don't know what happened out there, but I know the man flying that plane. I keep thinking about you and us together again. You once said winter makes everything still. Come home when you can. I miss the stillness.

He folded it gently and tucked it into his pocket, feeling the paper's edge against his palm like an anchor, just as the orderly arrived.

"Captain Whitaker," the man said. "Priority reassignment. Stateside. Transport in three days."

No grand speech followed. Jack gathered the crew that night.

"We've got orders," he said simply. "We're going home."

No cheers. Just silence. A long one. Then Murphy let out a low whistle.

"Feels strange," said Sayers.

"Yeah," Jack nodded, eyes turned west toward the jungle. "It does."

But the wind was shifting. And even ghosts moved on.

CHAPTER FIVE
THE LONG WAY HOME

The airstrip buzzed with idling engines and shouted orders, but to Jack Whitaker, it was a distant hum. The war was finally behind him—mostly. He stood near the edge of the field, hands in his pockets, watching the haze curl off the jungle, already feeling its pull on his thoughts. Part of him wondered if the jungle was still holding onto pieces of them. A C-47 sat warming up nearby, its propellers ticking slowly to life. Not their old bird—not Peto's Key—but another gray-backed sky mule, ready to carry what was left of them home. The morning air was heavy with dust and jet fuel, each breath tasting like the end of something he wasn't sure he wanted to end.

One by one, the others found him.

Sayers arrived first, grease still under his fingernails, sleeves rolled up. He looked like he'd just stepped out of a motor pool, and maybe he had.

"She's not our bird," Sayers said, nodding toward the plane. "But she'll fly."

Jack gave a quiet nod. "That's all we need."

Sayers smirked. "Not all we want, though."

LeClair came next, limping slightly, an unlit cigarette tucked between his teeth. He carried his duffel like a man shouldering more than weight.

"Still feels wrong," he muttered, his eyes on the jungle's edge. "Leaving without her. She was family."

Jack didn't ask who he meant. Peto's Key was still out there, somewhere in the trees. Part of her, part of them, left behind.

"You think she's still holding together?" Jack asked.

LeClair shrugged. "Long as the jungle lets her."

Murphy strolled up last, twirling a battered playing card between his fingers.

"Well," he said, "they're finally sending the riffraff home. About time."

Jack chuckled. "You figure out where you're headed?"

"Stateside," Murphy said. "Not sure where after that. Might head west. Heard there's poker in Reno and sunlight in California. What about you?"

"Back to Michigan," Jack said, but his voice was distant, as if the word itself was slipping through his fingers. "Tommy too. Petoskey is waiting."

Murphy grinned. "God help it."

A short silence followed. Not awkward—just full.

LeClair broke it. "We made it, didn't we?"

Jack nodded. "Somehow."

Murphy pulled something from his jacket pocket—an old compass, cracked and blackened from the crash.

"Found this in my bag," he said, handing it to Jack. "Figured you ought to keep it. Not for flying. Just… remembering."

Jack took it, thumbing the lid open. The needle spun once, then settled.

"Thanks," he said.

Murphy tapped it lightly. "Points home, even if home's nowhere on the map."

They moved toward the waiting transport, duffels slung, boots thudding on the packed dirt. As they neared the stairs, Jack paused, turning back.

Tommy stood by the edge of the tent row, glove tucked under his arm, baseball nestled in the pocket. His hands were still healing, still stiff, but the young man who had sat on the jungle floor, eyes wide with fear, was not the same. He stood tall now, a boy grown into a man, whether he was ready or not.

"You ready?" Jack asked.

Tommy nodded. "Feels strange. Going home."

"Yeah," Jack said. "It does."

Tommy hesitated. "You think we'll still know the place?"

Jack smiled faintly, though it didn't reach

his eyes. "If it's changed, we'll just make it ours again."

They walked together toward the plane.

As the engines roared louder, each man gave his goodbye.

LeClair pulled Jack into a quick hug. "You ever head south, look me up. I'll teach you how to fish for cat down in the bayou."

Sayers shook Jack's hand with a firm grip. "Still owe you for getting us down in one piece."

Murphy tipped an invisible hat. "If you ever get bored of quiet skies, find me. I'll deal you in."

Jack gave a faint smile. "I just might."

The ramp clanked underfoot as he and Tommy climbed aboard. They found seats near the window. The jungle was already fading from view.

"Do you think people back home will understand?" Tommy asked.

Jack shook his head. "No. But that's not their fault."

Tommy looked down at the glove in his lap. "I feel like we're bringing ghosts with us."

Jack looked out the window. "We are.

But maybe they'll rest easier where the sky's quieter."

For a long moment, they just listened to the engines build, the low rumble becoming a steady roar. Jack's fingers closed around Murphy's compass in his pocket, feeling its weight. Somewhere ahead lay Michigan. Somewhere else lay whatever came next.

The engines roared. The wheels lifted. And Burma dropped away beneath them.

Through the haze, the jungle's green faded into cloud, and then into nothing at all—but Jack knew it was still back there, waiting. Some places never really let you go. And some pieces of us stay, buried deep, no matter how far we run.

The crew of Peto's Key flew westward, scattered to the winds, each carrying pieces of a story only they would ever fully understand.

But some part of them would always circle back to that wrecked bird in the jungle—and to each other.

CHAPTER SIX
THE WEIGHT OF WHAT REMAINS – BURMA 1981

Burma, 1981. Decades had passed, but the jungle remained, holding its secrets, its silence thick and heavy. And it offered up what it had once buried. The wreck was the same, half-forgotten and half-swallowed by nature's embrace. Vines coiled through the torn fuselage. Roots cracked through buckled aluminum. Moss spread like velvet over every surface, softening metal long since surrendered to rot and time. Only the tail number—half-swallowed by rust and leaves—hinted at the ghost of a name, the memory of a machine.

Dr. Evelyn Hart stepped over a fallen tree

limb, ducking beneath a curtain of damp leaves. Behind her, the Smithsonian Air and Space Museum recovery team lingered near the edge of the clearing, their equipment clunky but determined—canvas packs, coiled rope, and a tripod-mounted 35mm camera scanning the wreck through a slow manual sweep.

She adjusted her wide-brimmed hat, feeling the weight of the decades that had passed since this plane had last been in the air. It wasn't just metal she was looking at; it was the ghost of those who had flown it. Each inch of rust, each piece of torn fabric, seemed to carry the weight of the past, a history buried in the jungle's depths. "Looks like a C-47," she said, quietly reverent. "World War II model. Early build."

Her assistant, Miguel, circled the wing with caution, snapping photos as he went. "Fuselage is mostly intact. Still has the forward structure. And… here--" He ran a gloved hand along a faint band of white and black. "Invasion stripes. Faded, but they're here."

"Could've been a Hump run," Evelyn said. "Hundreds went down in this stretch—bad terrain, worse weather. The war moved on, but the jungle didn't."

Miguel crouched and tapped a notebook. "This matches the location the bush pilot reported. Said he spotted something shiny cutting through the canopy."

Evelyn nodded. "Took three months of paperwork just to get clearance to hike in here."

Inside the cargo bay, they moved slowly—hands brushing aside cobwebs and scattered jungle debris. The hold smelled of mold, wet leather, and time. Rusted tie-downs still clung to the floor. One wall bore the faded stencil of a weight limit and a nearly illegible warning in red: NO SMOKING WITHIN 10 FEET.

Near the rear door, Evelyn paused. A canvas strap hung from a hook, frayed but still fastened—like someone had stepped away and forgotten to undo it.

She frowned. "Whoever flew this didn't go easy."

"No sign of fire," Miguel noted. "Could've been a controlled landing. Looks like they walked away."

Evelyn stepped carefully toward the cockpit, her boots crunching over cracked Plexiglas. The jungle had seeped inside, creeping through seams and shattered windows. The controls were pitted and half-rotted, but the yoke was still there, crusted in mildew and lichen. She didn't touch it. Not yet.

Then she noticed the panel beneath the co-pilot's seat—partially open. Curious, she knelt and gently pulled it back. The metal groaned in protest.

Inside, tucked in a rusty corner of what might once have been a toolbox, was something small. Paper. Worn, water-damaged, but unmistakable.

A photograph.

Evelyn eased it free and held it to the light filtering through the trees. A woman, smiling. Dark hair pinned back, eyes focused just off camera. The edges were curled, the ink had bled in places, but the feeling was still there. Someone had cared enough to keep this close. Evelyn held it up to the light, her heart briefly constricting. The photograph seemed to pulse with quiet significance, as if it carried the weight of someone's entire world. She had seen this look before—eyes full of love, of longing. She'd seen it in the families who came searching for lost loved ones.

Miguel stepped beside her. "Family?"

"Maybe." Evelyn's voice dropped, softened by the weight of it. "Could be a wife. Girlfriend. Someone who mattered. Someone who was waiting for an answer."

She slid the photo carefully into a wax paper envelope. "We tag everything. Catalog it before we move anything. This stays with the wreck until we know where it belongs."

Miguel nodded. "You think this one's worth the effort? It's in rough shape."

Evelyn looked once more at the plane—its bones exposed, its secrets clutched tight.

"I don't know," she said. "But it feels like she's been waiting."

A breeze stirred the leaves, shifting shadows across the wing.

The jungle did not let go easily.

Even after the initial clearing was cut, vines began to crawl back over the wreck's battered shell within days. Roots gripped the landing gear like anchors. Mud threatened to swallow everything left behind. But still, the recovery team pressed on.

Each piece of the aircraft was tagged and measured. The wings, sheared at the root, had to be sawed into transportable lengths. The fuselage—crushed at the nose, mostly intact along the spine—was reinforced with scaffolding, then lifted, inch by inch, with rigged pulleys and sweat.

At night, the team slept in canvas tents pitched between tree trunks. Lanterns burned long after dinner, casting gold light on maps, manifests, and field logs. The wreck had begun to speak—but not clearly. Not yet.

Inside the stripped fuselage, mildew and rust gave way to clues: faded stencils in English, a single navigation chart folded beneath a rotted bench, a cracked leather headset.

They didn't speak of the name of the plane. Because there wasn't one. Not yet.

The tail number had been scorched and nearly erased by time. Letters peeled away, digits twisted. All they knew was that it had gone down in the 1940s, likely during the war. The flight manifest, if one ever existed, had never made it back.

No one on the team dared guess at who had flown it, or why it had ended here, swallowed by jungle.

When the helicopter came—an old Hind transport chartered from a private firm—it hovered just long enough to lift the heaviest section skyward. The sound shattered the jungle's hush. Birds scattered like shrapnel. Then it was gone.

The rest was moved slowly by foot and river.

Two weeks later, the crates arrived at the Smithsonian's Garber Restoration Facility in Maryland. The hangar, cool and dry, felt a world away from the thick, green silence of Burma.

Technicians began their work immediately brushing away rot, treating corrosion, logging every artifact into a database still written mostly by hand.

"Tail number's fragmented," said one of the restoration leads, studying a scrap of rear fuselage. "Could be a dozen different registries."

Miguel, now clean-shaven and still recovering from dengue fever, peered over his shoulder.

"We may have to wait for forensic paint analysis. Or we cross-reference structural details—bulkhead shape, rivet pattern. That might narrow it down."

Evelyn nodded but said nothing. Her thoughts lingered on the photograph now stored in a humidity-controlled drawer.

She had seen the look in that woman's eyes before—not just captured on film, but in the expressions of families who had once come to claim personal effects, hoping for answers. For them, the wrecks had been graves, but Evelyn knew they held more than just bones and metal. They told stories. And stories, even lost ones, always found their way back.

"What do you think?" Miguel asked one evening, as they stood beside the stripped fuselage under the cold hum of fluorescent light. "Do you think we'll ever know who they were?"

Evelyn took her time answering, staring at the wreck as if the plane itself might whisper the answers.

"I think," she said finally, "some aircraft carry more than cargo. Sometimes they carry memories—forgotten, stories, fragments of lives. And those memories... they find a way to keep speaking."

Outside, snow had begun to fall—soft flakes whispering against the hangar roof.

The war was decades gone. The jungle, too, was half a world away.

But Evelyn couldn't shake the feeling that, in the bones of the old plane, something still waited. Not just stories. Something unfinished. Perhaps that's what these wrecks were: echoes of lives interrupted, their stories cut short. And in their decay, they found a way to speak again. Time hadn't erased them. Time had only held them.

CHAPTER SEVEN
SHE WAITED

Garber Restoration Facility – Maryland, 1983

Two winters had passed since the crates arrived from Burma, since the snow whispered against the Garber hangar's roof and the jungle's silence gave way to restoration.

The air inside was dry and smelled faintly of oil and lacquer. Overhead fluorescents buzzed quietly, casting long reflections on the polished panels. In the far corner, someone swept metal shavings into a tray, the sound echoing through the hangar like distant footsteps.

The tail number remained a question mark. Too much of it had been lost to time and tropics. Researchers and curators logged every part and structural quirk, but none of the serial numbers led anywhere definitive. The aircraft, though whole again, still bore no name.

But she had a presence.

Visitors to the facility—veterans, volunteers, student docents—often paused before her, silent for a few moments longer than they did at other exhibits. She stirred something. Something familiar. Something that made the air feel thick with unspoken memories.

The photograph remained the only personal clue. Stored under archival glass in the facility's main office, it had been digitally restored and cataloged. Still, no one had identified the woman with the quiet smile and steady gaze. Her image had traveled through veterans' newsletters, aviation groups, even a Smithsonian magazine feature—no replies.

Dr. Evelyn Hart walked the length of the aircraft one final time before the crew wheeled it toward the loading bay. Her gloved hand skimmed the smooth curve of the fuselage. Evelyn remembered the first time she saw the wreck half-buried in jungle rot—its ribs exposed, its silence suffocating. Now, restored under polished lights, the plane felt almost unfamiliar. But the weight she carried hadn't lightened. Not until she knew who had flown her. And who they'd left behind.

"You carried them far," she murmured. "Let's carry you a little farther."

The aircraft was loaded onto a military flatbed truck, escorted by a support team bound for Andrews Air Force Base. There, it would join a national tour—a traveling airshow and educational exhibit celebrating the unsung haulers of World War II. The workhorses, the sky mules, the C-47s that ferried men and supplies across war-torn skies.

Over the next year, the plane touched down in cities across the country—Dallas, Salt Lake City, Chicago, Dayton, San Diego. Children climbed into her belly and peered out the side windows. Veterans ran their hands along the riveted panels. Some stood quietly beside her, hands in pockets, eyes distant.

In Dallas, a woman touched the fuselage and whispered a name—was it hers, or someone lost in the same war? In Dayton, a former loadmaster sat inside her cargo hold for nearly an hour, silent and unmoving. He ran his hands over the cold metal, as though hoping to summon the faces of those who had once walked this path. Some visitors returned twice, their eyes lingering longer than the next visitor, their hands tracing the rivets as if to say goodbye to something they hadn't realized they'd missed. Some faces were softer, some harder, but all of them came with a story—a ghost, a memory, a moment of the past buried in time.

Still, the plane no longer whispered. She only waited.

It was in Kalamazoo that everything began to change.

At the Air Zoo Aerospace & Science Museum, tucked into the heart of Michigan aviation country, the plane drew unusual attention. Museum staff noted a surge in veteran visitors, many lingering in the hangar long after closing. A few asked to see the photograph.

Then came the call.

"We'd like to house her permanently," said the voice on the other end of the line—Beth

Lambert, director of curation at the Air Zoo. "She belongs here. Our board is unanimous. If the Smithsonian is willing to loan her, we'll build the exhibit around her story. Even if we don't know all of it."

Evelyn, who had overseen the plane's recovery and restoration since day one, leaned back in her chair. The warbird had traveled far. Now, maybe, she was coming home.

Within six months, the loan was approved. The aircraft was flown—strapped inside a cargo hold, wingless once again—to Michigan.

She was reassembled in a climate-controlled hangar at the Air Zoo. A permanent exhibit rose around her: a jungle diorama with real vegetation, digital panels telling the story of wartime aviation, and at its center, a glass case with one photograph and a placard that read:

Recovered in Burma. Restored in Maryland. Identity unknown.

Some aircraft carry more than cargo.

People came. More stories were shared. Some whispered memories stirred.

But still, no name.

CHAPTER EIGHT
THE ONE I LEFT BEHIND

The C-47 was about to settle into its final resting place—an exhibit at the Air Zoo—just as the past was about to collide with the present in the quiet of Northern Michigan.

Captain Jack Whitaker sat in his favorite armchair at Independent Village, the familiar creak of the seat echoing in the stillness of the small room. The scent of coffee, floor polish, and well-worn paperbacks lingered in the air, mixing with the lazy hum of the ceiling fans, which barely stirred the warm June air. On the television, the Detroit Tigers stumbled through another inning.

Jack's posture was still proud, though his once broad frame had thinned with the years. A wool blanket lay across his knees, and the soft ticking of the wall clock filled the room with an almost rhythmic comfort. Beside him, Tommy Dillard shifted in his chair, adjusting his walker with a grunt. The old leather glove from Burma swung gently from one of its handles, its smooth, laces still intact. Tommy tapped Jack lightly on the arm.

"You think they'll blow it in the eighth again?" Tommy asked, a faint half-smile playing at the corner of his lips.

Jack didn't take his eyes off the screen. "Depends on whether they remember how to bunt."

The two men settled into a comfortable silence, worn smooth with the years. It was the kind of quiet shared between old friends—no need for words when the bond was already understood. The Tigers were losing. Again. But neither of them had come to the lounge for the game. It was the ritual, the simple comfort of watching something familiar unfold, even if the outcome was never in doubt.

As the commercial break ended, the channel shifted to a local news segment, framed by bright red, white, and blue banners. A young anchor beamed into the camera with a wide smile.

"This Fourth of July don't miss one of the most anticipated events of the summer. Harbor Springs Airport is proud to host the Wings of Freedom Flyover, an aerial tribute to the brave men and women of the Second World War. Headlining the show—a fully restored World War II C-47 Skytrain, flown in from the Smith-sonian archives..."

Tommy shifted in his chair, sensing the change in Jack's posture. Jack leaned forward, the weight of decades pressing into the moment.

"The aircraft—still officially unidentified but known only by its partial markings—has been touring airshows across the country as part of a Smithsonian and Air Zoo initiative to honor the lost air crews of the Pacific theater. Its final summer appearance will be right here, before she's retired to permanent exhibition. During restoration, crews found a black-and-white pho-tograph tucked behind the cockpit panel—a mys-tery woman, thought to be a personal keepsake from one of the original crew."

The camera shifted to slow-motion footage of the C-47 banking through golden sunlight, its wings catching the sky. But it wasn't the plane that held Jack's gaze. It was the image that followed.

A woman in grayscale, her smile wide and knowing, her eyes just off-camera, as though caught mid-laugh. Her hair pinned back the way he remembered. The edges of the photograph worn and curling, as though time had tried to erase her, but failed.

Sarah.

Jack didn't move. His lips parted, then closed again. He leaned forward slightly, as if trying to pull something from the depths of his memory, something long buried, now rising to the surface.

"Jack?" Tommy asked softly, sensing the shift in his friend.

"That's her," Jack whispered, barely above a murmur. "That's the one I left in the toolbox. The day we went down."

The memory hit him in a wave—the rain on the day the plane had gone down, cold and relentless. The tremble in his fingers as he tucked her photo beneath the wrench roll, a small act he hadn't thought twice about at the time. He had promised himself he'd come back for it. For her.

Now, somehow, the past had found its way back home before he ever did.

The Tigers returned from the commercial break, but neither man noticed.

Outside, sunlight filtered through the blinds, casting a soft glow on the dust motes drifting in the air. Jack didn't look away from the window as he spoke again, his voice quiet but certain.

"It's her. There's no doubt. The rivet line beneath the co-pilot window... the dent in the starboard wing root. That's Peto's Key."

Tommy stared at Jack, the weight of the moment settling over him like a heavy fog. "You thinking about calling the Air Zoo?"

Jack turned, his eyes steady now, a quiet resolve behind them. "Not to visit. I want to fly her. One last time."

Tommy blinked, taken aback by the words. "Fly her? Jack, we've got bad knees, blood thinners, and a bedtime alarm. They won't even let us use the elevator unsupervised."

Jack's crooked grin spread across his face, familiar, mischievous. "Then we don't ask."

Tommy snorted, shaking his head. "You want to steal the plane?"

"Borrow. Reclaim," Jack said with a shrug. "She's ours, Tommy. Always was. If they won't let us take her up proper, we find a way. Just once. Before we can't."

Tommy's eyes dropped to the glove in his lap. His fingers closed around it—the same glove he had caught hell with over the Himalayas. The weight of it, of the past, settled in his chest as he thought about it all.

"You really think we could pull it off?" Tommy asked, his voice quieter now, weighed down by the possibility.

"I do. But we'll need the crew."

Jack didn't respond right away. His eyes were distant, staring at the television, though he wasn't seeing it. The silence stretched, broken only by the ticking clock and the faint hum of the TV. Finally, his voice came, quiet but firm. "Some of them won't be there."

Tommy gave a slow nod. "But the ones who are... That's enough."

Jack nodded in agreement. He pushed himself up from the chair with a soft grunt, the years weighing on him more than the blanket across his knees. He moved to the nightstand, opened the drawer, and retrieved a battered black address book. The corners were soft, curling, held together by tape and memory.

He placed it gently between them, sitting back down slowly, almost reverently. This book—these names—represented the crew of Peto's Key, the men who had survived it all. And they were all still alive, despite the years, despite the distance, and despite the ghosts that followed them.

He flipped to the first circled name.

"Murphy," Jack said, tapping the faded line with a callused finger. "Traverse City now. Last I heard, he's still hustling poker nights at the Elks Lodge, talking his way out of parking tickets."

Tommy chuckled, a faint smile tugging at

his lips. "Murph could sell snow to a moose. He'll be game."

Jack turned a few more pages.

"Sayers," he said, his finger resting on the name. "Down in Dayton. Family man. Quiet. The kind of guy who'd fix your carburetor while you're still trying to find the hood latch."

"He's probably still got that belt pouch with half a toolbox in it," Tommy added, grinning. "Could fix a radio with a paperclip and a piece of gum."

Jack smiled, flicking the page. "LaClair. Billy. Louisiana. Still sends me a Christmas card with a fish on it. Always knew how to make folks like him."

Tommy's grin deepened. "You could drop Billy into a room full of strangers, and he'd come out with three new cousins and a barbecue invitation."

Jack stared at the last few entries, his finger tracing over names that no longer mattered. Some crossed out. Some circled in memory, but not in life. A silence settled between them, filled with the ghosts of those who couldn't make it.

He closed the book gently, laid it flat on the table, and tapped the cover softly, as if to steady himself.

"We get them back together," he said, voice thick with resolve. "One more mission. No brass. No briefings."

He looked out the window, the sunlight dancing on the bay just right. "Just sky."

CHAPTER NINE
REASSEMBLY

The news had aired just the night before, but Jack was already moving like a man with orders in hand. The black address book lay open before him, a topographical map of his past. A slant of golden light pooled at his feet, while his coffee sat cooling, untouched.

The photo of Sarah still burned in his mind—her smile behind a war-scarred instrument panel. Peto's Key had made it home. It felt like a message. A call to finish something left undone.

From the next room, Tommy's shuffle echoed, slower than it used to be, but still purposeful. He leaned in the doorway, mug in hand.

"You making calls already?" Tommy asked.

Jack didn't look up. "Murphy's first. He's the one who never really landed."

Tommy huffed a laugh. "If he's still breathing, he's bluffing someone out of gas money."

Jack picked up the phone and dialed from memory.

Three rings.

"Murphy's Automotive and Games of Chance," a gravelly voice answered. "If you're selling insurance or asking about debts, you've got the wrong number."

Jack smiled. "Still running the same racket?"

Three rings.

"Murphy's Automotive and Games of Chance," a gravel-rough voice answered. "If you're selling insurance or asking about debts, you've got the wrong number."

Jack smiled. "Still running the same racket?"

A pause.

"…Jack Whitaker? I'll be damned. You're not calling me from the afterlife, are you?"

"Not yet."

Across the table, Tommy raised a brow. "Tell him the Tigers still can't bunt."

Jack relayed the message.

Murphy barked out a laugh. "God, that takes me back. What's this about? You two break out of your retirement home and need bail money?"

Jack's tone softened. "It's the plane, Murph. We saw her. Peto's Key. They brought her back. Fully restored. Final flyover's right here in Michigan."

There was a pause. Then Murphy's voice dropped, all the mischief stripped away.

"You sure?"

"Positive," Jack said. "Same dent in the starboard wing root. Even found the photo of Sarah. The one I left behind."

Tommy leaned forward. "Your Sarah never left Jack. She waited here. That old bird just took sixty years to catch up."

A longer silence. Then Murphy said, with quiet resolve: "I'll bring the dice."

Jack nodded, flipping to the next name. "Sayers," he muttered.

Tommy snorted. "Bet he's already packed a wrench and a flask of WD-40."

Dayton.

Jack dialed again. A clear, clipped voice answered. "Sayers."

A pause. "Jack?"

"Still breathing. Still grumpy."

Sayers gave a short, rusty laugh. "I'll be damned. Last time I heard from you, Billy was trying to smoke trout on the engine block."

Jack chuckled. "We saw her, Sayers. The plane. Peto's Key."

Sayers didn't respond at first. Then: "I dreamed about her last week. Don't know why. Thought I was back under that wing, wiring the comms with a busted soldering iron."

"She's flying again," Jack said. "And we're putting the crew back together. One last run."

Sayers took a long breath. "I'll need a couple days to square away my garage… but yeah. I'm in."

Tommy leaned over. "Make sure he brings that ratchet set. The one older than we are."

"I never leave home without it," Sayers replied dryly. "And tell Tommy I still owe him for cracking that fuel gauge in '44."

They all laughed.

One name left.

Jack turned to the final name—Billy LaClair, Louisiana. Loadmaster. Charmer. The kind of man who could hitch a ride on a Tuesday and end up cooking gumbo at someone else's family reunion by Friday.

Jack dialed. The line clicked, and a familiar voice answered, thick with Southern drawl.

"LaClair here. If this is Jack Whitaker, you're about thirty years overdue and two whiskies short of proper manners."

Jack laughed. "Still got the timing of a parade, Billy."

"Well, I'll be," Billy said, voice warming instantly. "Captain Whitaker. Ain't heard your voice since that busted reunion in '79. What's the good word?"

Jack's tone steadied. "The plane. Peto's Key. She's back. Same dent under the wing. Last airshow's here in Michigan."

A beat of silence.

"Thought she went down for good," Billy said. "Swore if anything came back from that jungle, it wouldn't be her."

"She's flying again," Jack said. "And we're getting the crew back together."

Billy's voice dropped low. "I'm in. I don't even need to pack. Just tell me where to show up."

From across the table, Tommy leaned in. "And bring something better than that powdered coffee you used to swear by. I've had shoe polish that tasted smoother."

Billy chuckled. "Tell Tommy not to worry. I've got fresh catfish on ice, a bottle of the good stuff, and three stories so wild I can't even tell them in church."

"Same old Billy," Jack said, smiling.

Jack placed the phone down, the faint click of the receiver settling in the quiet room. He looked at the black address book in front of him, the names now more than just memories—they were the crew, the men who had once been part of something larger, something they'd all survive. And now, they would all be together again.

Tommy, still holding the baseball mitt, sat back in his chair, the seams worn smooth from years of use. It was a piece of their past, just like the men they'd once been. But even now, with the years between them, the bond they shared hadn't wavered.

"We're really doing this, huh?" Tommy's voice was soft, but there was a steady resolve in it.

Jack nodded slowly. "Yeah, we are."

Tommy's fingers tightened around the glove in his lap. "I'll tell you one thing, Jack. No matter how much time passed, some things don't change. And some people—" He paused, his eyes fixed on the glove. "They never go anywhere."

Jack looked at him, a faint, tired smile forming on his lips. "No, they don't." He took a deep breath and let it out, looking out the window where the daylight still danced across the bay. It felt like a promise. A way forward.

"Let's make it count," Tommy said, his voice stronger now, more certain.

Jack turned back to the table, his hand resting on the old address book. He closed it gently and tapped the cover. "One last time, Tommy. One last time in the sky."

Tommy nodded, the silence between them

comfortable now, full of understanding and unspoken words. Jack stood, his movements slower than before, but still purposeful. He walked toward the window, staring out at the quiet world beyond.

"This time," Jack said quietly, "we're doing it for us. For all of us."

Tommy's eyes followed him, and for a moment, the room seemed to hold its breath. Then, with a soft chuckle, Tommy added, "We never did things the easy way, did we?"

Jack smiled and turned back to him. "Guess that's what makes us who we are."

He glanced at the address book once more, then back at the window, where the light shifted gently across the water. The road ahead was uncertain, but it was theirs to take.

Together.

With a deep breath, Jack turned toward the door, ready for whatever would come next.

CHAPTER TEN
WRINKLED, READY, AND RECKLESS

By the end of the week, they started to arrive. Old boots, louder engines, and enough baggage—emotional and otherwise—to fill a hangar.

Naturally, Murphy was the first to arrive. You didn't spend a lifetime bluffing poker hands and dodging parking tickets without learning how to beat traffic.

Just outside town, Independent Village sat quiet and orderly—a modest building with wide porches, trimmed hedges, and a lawn that whispered of routine, where the grass stayed short and the conversations long. Then came the rattling crescendo of a battered Crown Vic with mismatched hubcaps, clattering into the parking lot like a pocketful of nickels. The engine coughed twice, then fell silent with a final wheeze. From the passenger side, the door flung open and out popped a whirlwind in cutoffs and high-tops.

"Pop says you owe him a quarter tank of gas and at least one apology," the girl announced before the dust even settled.

Captain Jack Whitaker leaned on his cane at the front entrance, watching with one brow raised.

The girl marched up, hand on her hip, chin tilted defiantly. "You the famous Captain? Name's Riley. I'm Murphy's designated driver, unpaid therapist, and general life manager. Try not to faint from the awesomeness."

Tommy, seated just behind Jack, coughed into his hand to hide a laugh.

From the driver's seat, Murphy emerged, slower and creakier, adjusting his suspenders and squinting toward the porch. "Ignore her. I told her you were all hard of hearing and prone to naps."

"And I told you, if you call me 'kiddo' again, I'm throwing your hearing aids in the lake."

Jack stepped forward and extended his hand. "Welcome to Independent Village."

"Independent, huh?" Riley looked around at the trimmed hedges and sleepy windows. "Seems like everyone here's on a schedule and a stool softener."

Murphy groaned. "She's charming, isn't she?"

But Jack was smiling. "More than half the nurses here are afraid of me. She'll fit right in."

Inside, rooms had been set aside for the arriving crew—small guest suites usually reserved for family visits or the rare out-of-state shuffleboard tournament. Jack and Tommy had arranged everything down to the guest passes and welcome kits: snacks, aspirin, and a laminated schedule of cafeteria pie offerings.

Sayers arrived next, in a beige sedan that looked as dependable as he was. He'd retired twice—once from the phone company and once from small engine repair—and had built his own ham radio setup in the garage. His hands were slower now but still callused from years of use.

"I brought my wrench set," he said,

unloading a canvas bag from the trunk. "Figured I'd better bring it just in case."

Tommy leaned against the doorframe and chuckled. "You didn't think we'd ask you to fix the elevator, did you?"

Sayers shrugged. "Didn't want to take the chance."

Billy LaClair was the last to roll in—driving a camper painted with a mural of a marlin leaping into a setting sun. The Florida plates read: GONEFISHN.

"Hope y'all got room for one more old fool and a cooler full of catfish," Billy called, arms wide as he stepped down. His knees cracked like popcorn. "Smoked it myself. And if anyone says they don't like Cajun spices, they're sleeping outside. And if you can't handle the heat, the porch is yours."

Billy was never a pilot, but he'd logged more miles in a jump seat than most co-pilots saw in their careers. His voice still had that easy drawl that made strangers trust him and old friends feel younger.

The jokes came easy, but beneath them was something heavier – earned and understood.

"Billy, remember that time you made us all take a 'shortcut' through the jungle?" Jack asked with a smile. "We nearly lost the plane—and the crew—on that one."

Billy grinned. "What can I say? A man's gotta trust his gut. The fact that it was a little off doesn't mean I was wrong."

The banter flew fast and thick, but as they stood there, Jack let it wash over him. Laughter. Sarcasm. Bad knees and worse jokes. They were here. They came. And for the first time in a long time, he didn't feel like time had slipped past him. It wasn't just a reunion—it was reclamation.

Jack watched as his old crew gathered beneath the portico, the rhythm of their banter already falling into place. It wasn't just a reunion—it was reclamation. Time had taken its toll, but not their bond.

Riley leaned in toward her grandfather. "So these are the guys? The ones from your stories?"

Murphy nodded. "Yeah, kiddo. These are the ones who came home."

She looked around at the weathered faces and faded ball caps. "They don't look like much." And as the men joked and swatted each other on the shoulder, something flickered behind her teasing grin—recognition. These weren't just old guys – they were history in motion. Survivors of a world most people only read about.

Murphy grinned. "Neither does a weather balloon till it climbs high enough."

Jack caught Riley's gaze, amusement playing behind his eyes. "You planning to keep us in line?"

"Please," Riley said, arms crossed. "I am not babysitting. I am supervising. You're all one bad idea away from making the evening news."

Jack laughed. "Then stick close. We're just getting started."

CHAPTER ELEVEN
OPERATION GEEZER RECON

By mid-morning, Jack's kitchenette looked more like a war room than a retirement apartment. A folding card table groaned under maps, newspapers, airshow flyers, and a battered Rand McNally Road atlas. In the corner, the coffee maker sputtered like it was running on diesel fumes.

"First rule of operations," Jack said, tapping a calloused finger against the table, "no good soldier flies blind."

Tommy nodded, pushing his glasses up the bridge of his nose. "We don't know the layout, we don't know the crowd, and we sure as hell don't know how close we can get."

"Or how long she'll be out in the open," Sayers added, adjusting the Velcro strap on his wrist brace. "Figured I'd better bring it just in case." He eyed the maps with a practiced, quiet intensity. "They'll probably rope her off with the rest of the warbirds. Might already be under canvas."

Murphy leaned closer to the map, chewing on the end of a ballpoint pen. "We need boots on the ground. Find out where they're staging the vintage planes. Confirm it's her. Confirm she's flyable."

Jack didn't say it out loud, but they all knew: some missions only work when the wheels leave the ground.

Billy chuckled. "You make it sound like we're robbing a bank."

"Same rules apply," Jack muttered. "Only thing more dangerous than a green pilot is a crowd full of tourists with disposable cameras."

The door creaked open, and Riley swept in, balancing two cafeteria trays and a notebook under one arm.

"Rations secured," she said, setting the trays down. "And your bingo cards are stashed in the red bin by the piano, in case tactical boredom strikes."

"Appreciate it," Billy said, reaching for a biscuit. "We were just planning a low-key infiltration of a civilian event."

"Oh, that's cute," Riley replied, scanning the cluttered table. "So, Operation Geezer Recon is a go?"

"Watch it," Murphy said. "Last guy who joked like that woke up with his garden gnome holding a white flag."

Jack gestured toward the empty chair. "You want in, or just here to roast us?"

Riley didn't answer right away. She dropped into the seat, flipped open her spiral notebook, and set it down like she was arming a grenade. "I'm in," she said. "Already been scouting."

Jack raised an eyebrow. "Go on."

She flipped to a page marked with arrows, doodles, and coffee stains. "I called the Chamber of Commerce. They mailed out flyers. One of the secretaries said the viewing area has bleachers on the west side, fenced in. Vendors line up just past the security gate. And there's a hot dog stand called The Flying Frank—"

"You're kidding," Murphy said, smirking.

"Nope. Real thing." Riley tapped her notes. "They've got a retired air traffic controller doing commentary over loudspeakers. Weather is supposed to hold—sunny, light breeze from the northeast. Press and vendors get in early."

Jack folded his arms. "You get all that from a secretary?"

"She liked my voice," Riley shrugged. "And I told her I was helping coordinate for a group of... honored veterans."

Billy chuckled. "She ain't wrong."

Jack gave a short nod. "Nice work. That gives us our window."

"We confirm it's her," Murphy said. "See how she's being handled. Who's around her. If they've got plans to fly or just pose for pictures."

Sayers pointed to one of the maps. "Public parking's over here. Staff gate's here. If it's a proper setup, they'll have her parked with the rest of the warbirds near the hangars."

"We'll need someone in early," Murphy said. "Before they hang a banner over her nose."

"I can pass for media," Riley offered. "With

the right badge and clipboard, I'll get in early, maybe talk my way up close."

Tommy gave her a sideways look. "You're volunteering for recon?"

"I'm just saying," she added, "if subtlety's the goal, I've got the edge over the usual PR folks."

There was a pause.

Then Murphy raised his coffee cup. "She's one of us."

"She's something alright. One of us," Tommy muttered with a grin.

Billy leaned back, eyeing her over his cup. "Talks fast, throws out static, and jams half the signal but somehow gets through."

He pointed. "That's your callsign. Static."

Riley blinked. "Wait, seriously?"

Jack nodded. "Earn it tomorrow."

Riley cracked a smile. "I've had worse."

Tommy snorted. "Yeah? Like what?"

"Middle school. Long story. Involved a cafeteria tray and a very unfortunate sneeze."

Murphy leaned in. "Welcome aboard, Static."

Riley mock saluted. "Ready for recon, sir."

Jack stood and folded the map in front of him. "Alright. We move tomorrow. Eyes only. Quiet. No fuss."

"You do know this is just an airshow, right?" Tommy said. "Not Omaha Beach."

Jack grunted. "Last airshow I came back sunburned, blistered, and sixty bucks lighter thanks to a thermos I still regret."

The room fell into a quiet rhythm—marking maps, packing notes, sipping lukewarm coffee. On the wall behind Jack's desk, a photo was pinned crookedly above the light switch. A girl in a summer dress, smiling by the edge of a Michigan lake.

Sarah.

She was never on the flight deck, never near the C-47. But she had been there on every mission Jack flew, carried in a folded photo behind his flight log. She wasn't a crew member. She was the reason.

Jack caught the glance, then turned back to the others.

"If it's her," Billy asked quietly, "what then?"

Jack's voice dropped. "Then we take it one step at a time. Whatever comes next, we face it together."

They all nodded.

The crew was back.

And this time, they had Static on comms.

CHAPTER TWELVE
EYES ON TOMORROW

By dawn, Independence Village was already stirring. The sprinklers hadn't even kicked on, but Jack's crew was already rolling out—sore backs, stiff joints, and all. The mission was simple: get to the Harbor Springs Airport, confirm the plane, and get a full layout of the airshow grounds. In and out. No fuss.

Tommy slid into the back of Billy's camper, the marlin mural along its side catching the first light like a brag. Murphy rode shotgun, nursing a chipped thermos and squinting at road signs. Jack followed in Riley's rattling Crown Vic, the trunk loaded with folding chairs, a pair of binoculars, a paper map creased white at the folds, and enough Werther's Originals to launch a dentist's convention.

The Harbor Springs Airport wasn't built for spectacle. On a normal day, it served weekend hobby pilots, the occasional private jet, and a handful of wealthy summer residents who liked their martinis no more than ten minutes from the tarmac. But today, the airfield hummed with a different energy. Rows of cones marked off temporary parking, food vendors were setting up behind sagging tents, and security volunteers in oversized orange vests wandered around with clipboards and radios.

They parked in two rows back from the temporary security gate, where a vinyl banner flapped in the breeze:

WELCOME TO THE 4TH OF JULY HERITAGE WEEKEND!

WINGS OF FREEDOM

Jack stood quietly at the edge of the lot, arms crossed, eyes scanning the horizon.

"There she is," he murmured, like spotting an old friend across a crowded room.

Peto's Key.

Even half-covered by canvas and flanked by a gleaming P-51 Mustang and a rust-bucket B-25, she stood out—quiet and unmistakable. Like a half-whispered story. Like she'd been waiting for them.

"Still think we're just going to an airshow?" Jack asked, his voice low.

"Nope," Tommy said, eyes locked on the tail markings. "Not anymore."

Riley snapped a photo from behind her sunglasses. "Alright, Static reporting in. We're on the ground. Time to split up and get what we came for."

Billy nodded. "Let's figure out who's running the show, what their schedule looks like, and how close we can get without setting off any alarms."

Sayers tapped his watch. "We've got three hours before they start pushing the public in. Less if they move early."

"Then let's make it count," Jack said.

No one said it out loud, but they all felt it: this was the final dry run. Next time, it wouldn't be maps and murmurs—it'd be movement.

They moved like veterans who'd done this before—because they had. Not in airports or parades, but in jungles, skies, and airstrips halfway across the world. This was different. But the rhythm came back easy—eyes open, ears sharp, never walk in blind.

Billy wandered the perimeter near the rear fencing, counting security cameras, snapping photos of gates, and marking exits on a paper program folded like a field map.

"They're not watching the backside," he said later. "Too focused on crowd flow. If we need a soft entry, that service lane's our ticket."

Tommy, camera in hand, took a slow walk past the aircraft lineup. He posed as a casual tourist, but every click was deliberate—targeting wheels, tail numbers, any fuel connections or locks.

"Two birds still covered," he noted, handing Jack the camera. "But I got a clean angle on one of the engine cowlings. Those rivets match. That's her."

Sayers drifted toward the maintenance tent, all curiosity and slow steps. He struck up a conversation with a teenage volunteer refilling coolers.

"Fuel's on a truck, not a pump," he told the group later. "Arrives tomorrow morning. If she's got any gas left in her, it'll be just fumes. We'll need a plan for that."

Murphy chatted up the audio technician setting up speakers near the bleachers. A handshake and a shared coffee later, he'd walked away with a copy of the day's program.

"Opening remarks start at 10:15," he said. "Parachute jump at 10:30. Flyover window's just after noon. That gives us a sunrise-to-nine window, give or take. And if they shuffle the schedule? Less."

Meanwhile, Riley slipped past the vendors and made herself a fixture at the media check-in table. Her fake press badge passed with zero resistance.

"Vendor access is open until six," she reported, rejoining the others. "I scoped the rosters—some vintage aircraft are arriving late this afternoon. There's one C-47 on the manifest listed only by its tail number."

"It's not on any airshow database I could find," she added, "which means it's either a ghost or a wildcard."

Jack's eyes narrowed. "That could be our girl."

"Could be," Riley said. "Won't know until she's out in the open."

They regrouped at The Flying Frank, a red-and-white striped food truck parked near the bleacher section. The scent of grilled onions and sizzling sausage hung thick in the air. A hand-painted chalkboard listed The Wingman Special, Dogfight Chili Dog, and The C-47 Classic—two hot dogs with everything, chips, and a root beer.

Murphy already had one in hand when the others arrived. "You ever eat a hot dog with jet fuel in the air?" he said, chewing thoughtfully. "Brings out the mustard."

Jack rolled his eyes. "Try not to blow our cover."

Billy leaned against the truck, scanning the crowd. "Nothing suspicious near the hangars. A couple volunteers with clipboards, one guy in a jumpsuit who thinks he's Maverick."

Sayers pulled out a crumpled notepad. "Security's light. One uniformed sheriff. Mostly event staff. A few fences, nothing serious. Volunteers rotate every four hours. Graveyard shift's the lightest—if they even show up."

Tommy held up the disposable camera again. "Got a few snaps of the flightline. One of the tarps has shifted just enough—you can see her tailwheel assembly. It's her."

They all stood quiet for a moment, nursing drinks and glancing back toward the tarmac. Somewhere behind them, the announcer's microphone crackled to life for a sound check—a reminder the clock was ticking.

"Tomorrow's our only shot," Jack finally said. "We confirm tonight. First light tomorrow, we make our move."

Murphy nodded. "You bringing the keys or the wings?"

Jack cracked a grin. "Both."

Riley raised her cup. "To recon."

"To freedom," Billy added.

"Peto's Key," Jack said softly.

They clinked drinks and took a long pull.

Around them, the crowd buzzed with anticipation. Planes roared overhead. But the crew didn't look up. Their eyes were already on tomorrow—on the wings, the sky, and the narrow hours before the clock ran out.

CHAPTER THIRTEEN
THE LONGEST CHECKLIST

By mid-afternoon, Independent Village had shifted into full holiday mode—stars-and-stripes bunting on balcony rails, someone testing fireworks too early, and the smell of charcoal drifting through the halls. Flags flapped lazily in the breeze, radios played Glenn Miller next to Pat Benatar, and folding chairs lined up like troops awaiting orders.

But Jack's crew was already thinking beyond picnic tables and parades. Their mission clock was already ticking.

They rolled back in from Harbor Springs quiet and sunbaked, the Crown Vic trailing behind Billy's camper like a support vehicle. There was no chatter on the ride—just the weight of what they'd seen, and what it meant. The tailwheel was hers. The layout was sloppy. The window of opportunity was thin. They had one shot, and now they had to make it count.

Back at the Village, while the rest of the residents shuffled off to a red-white-and-blue bingo tournament in the rec hall, Jack's apartment had become a war room.

The kitchenette was cleared, a fan buzzed softly in the corner, and three folding chairs had been arranged in the center of the living room, angled just so—pilot, mechanic, and loadmaster. The old recliner had been repositioned—navigator's station by way of La-Z-Boy. A clipboard dangled from a standing lamp. An empty thermos had been duct-taped upright in front of the "pilot's seat" to simulate the yoke. Murphy had clipped an old aviator headset—held together by electrical tape—to the arm of the chair.

Sayers crouched nearby, wiring a salvaged toggle box built from a shortwave radio and what might've been part of a blender. "Won't transmit squat," he muttered, "but it clicks. That's something. Just like wiring comms under a tarp on that jungle strip in '44."

Jack hovered by the window, rolling a small brass compass between his fingers. Scratched, tarnished, and stamped on the underside with the initials P.K.—etched clumsily with a screwdriver somewhere in the Burmese jungle. It had pointed north out of Burma, west across oceans, and finally to this Michigan town. Somehow, it had always known the way.

Murphy spotted it and let out a soft grunt. "You held onto that thing?"

Jack didn't look away from the glass. "You gave it to me. When we were packing out. Said, 'If I don't make it back, at least one of us ought to know which way's home.'"

Murphy lowered himself into the loadmaster's seat with a creak. "Damn. Sounds like something I'd say."

Jack finally turned and offered the ghost of a smile. "You were always good with directions—especially when you were shoving crates of ammo out the door over the Hump."

Billy arrived last, holding a paper bag of

root beer bottles like contraband. "I got the essentials," he said. "And by essentials, I mean nostalgia and sugar."

Riley was already seated on the edge of the sofa, clipboard in hand, legs bouncing. "Okay, gentlemen. You wanted a dry run? Let's dry-run."

Jack stepped into his "cockpit." He adjusted the thermos yoke with ceremonial precision, like touching a relic. "Call it."

Riley flipped to her hand-drawn checklist and assumed her best ground-control voice. "Pre-flight checks. Sayers?"

Sayers raised a hand without looking up. "Switchboard reads green. We've got simulated power. About as good as the time I rewired a radio with a bayonet just to get us weather reports."

"Murphy?"

Murphy adjusted the old headset and squinted like he could still hear engine noise under the static. "Loadmaster ready. Doors latched, cargo clear. Just like the nights we dropped crates blind through cloud cover."

"Billy?"

Billy gave a thumbs-up and started leafing

through a maintenance manual that dated back to the Eisenhower administration. "Systems nominal. Rear door will close if we slam it hard enough. Same as Kunming."

"Tommy's not here," Riley said, "but he left a note: 'I know the charts, I know the route. Trust the navigator or don't fly.'"

Jack nodded once. "Engaging engines."

His hands moved across empty space like muscle memory had never left—throttle forward, mixture rich, switches flipped in sequence. His voice took on that quiet, focused edge they all remembered.

"Contact."

Billy answered reflexively, slipping into his old role. "Clear prop."

They all went quiet for a beat, as if waiting for the roar of twin engines to rise from the floor.

Jack closed his eyes and whispered, "She's alive."

The moment held.

Then he started talking through the checklist, and the crew followed. Gear up. Altitude set. Flaps to climb. Each called response brought something back—not just procedure but feeling. The thrill. The fear. The precision.

Billy leaned back, blinking hard. "You know, I can still smell the oil when you call 'gear up.' Like my hands just remember wrenching bolts tight before we hit a strip carved out of bamboo."

Sayers chuckled softly. "You always ran lean. Stank up the whole damn fuselage."

Murphy broke in, his voice low but sure. "We may be slower. Older. Some of us can't hear as well, can't see as far. But in this cockpit—" he looked around the chairs, the makeshift controls, the people— "we're still a crew."

Jack didn't say anything. He just reached into his shirt pocket and pinned a photo to the clipboard above the lamp. It was faded, frayed at the corners. Sarah—smiling on a beach back home. The same one he'd carried in the war. The one that rode every mission with him in a flight suit breast pocket.

Murphy saw it. Said nothing.

But Riley did. "She's beautiful," she whispered.

Jack nodded. "She waited. Just like the plane."

No one spoke for a while.

Outside, the Village bustled—music, grills, kids with sparklers, laughter echoing off stucco walls.

But inside, the only sound was memory.

Riley finally cleared her throat. "Alright, final sequence. Approach checklist. Let's fly her home."

Jack smiled now. A real one.

"Let's bring her in."

They worked through the last leg of the flight, voices overlapping calls and confirmations. Somewhere between pretend and real, something flickered to life. Not just the plan. Not just the plane.

But them.

The war might've ended decades ago, but they weren't done flying.

Not yet. The sun was starting to dip. One more sunset, and then they'd fly.

CHAPTER FOURTEEN
SMOKE AND MORNING LIGHT

Morning rose soft and warm, settling over northern Michigan somewhere between flag pancakes and Springsteen on the radio—another Fourth of July already humming with porch flags, parade routes, and patriotic purpose. By six, the sidewalks were alive with dog walkers in bandanas, joggers in red-white-and-blue sweatbands, and retirees deploying lawn chairs with military precision. Flags flapped from porch rails, bike baskets, and baby strollers. The air smelled like dew and grilled sausage, and Springsteen's voice—somewhere between Born to Run and Glory Days—drifted from a boombox balanced on a windowsill.

Jack watched it all from the corner of the

community garage, half-shadowed by the rising sun. He zipped up the old leather flight jacket—creased, faded, and stretched thin at the shoulders. The cuffs were frayed, the collar worn to suede, and a patch of the lining near the heart had long since split open. It had flown continents and crossed oceans with him, soaked in sweat over Burma and frozen stiff above the Aleutians. It didn't fit the way it once did—snug in the chest now, looser in the sleeves—but the weight of it still felt right. Like command. Like memory. Like something earned in the sky and carried through the years, even when the sky no longer called.

"Showtime," Murphy said beside him, tugging on a ball cap worn thin from decades of duty—and at least one grease fire.

Across the lot, Billy was stuffing the last of their supplies into the camper—tool kit, maps, a cooler full of sandwiches, and a suspicious number of extension cords. He tugged the tarp down tight and gave it a firm pat, like sealing a vault.

"Loaded and questionably legal," he muttered. "Just the way we like it."

"No questions, no answers," Sayers said, slamming the cargo hatch shut. He wore grease-stained coveralls and carried a wrench like it was a sidearm.

Tommy emerged from Jack's apartment with a duffel and a quiet, focused look. "Navigation maps, flashlights, and half a bag of Werther's. We ready?"

Riley leaned casually against the Crown Vic, the perfect picture of press credentials and purpose. She wore a fitted navy blazer over slacks, her hair pinned back with surgical neatness. A laminated press badge clipped to her lapel read MEDIA. A clipboard full of forged manifests rested on her hip. Her camera bag was slung over one shoulder, ready to sell the illusion.

Murphy gave a low whistle. "Well look at that. Static suits up and suddenly she's ready for the six o'clock news."

Sayers chuckled. "Sharp creases, clean collar. Reminds me of my first CO—only better posture and better hair."

Billy smirked. "She dresses like someone with a pension plan. What's that like?"

Riley didn't miss a beat. "Clean laundry and plausible credentials. You boys should try it sometime."

Tommy peered over the clipboard. "That badge laminated? Nice touch."

"Fake badge, real charm," she said. "I'm media now. Smile pretty and don't get in my shot."

Jack nodded. "You pull this off, and they'll think you're CBS. Hell, maybe you are."

"Only if they start paying," she replied.

The crew shared a soft laugh—just enough to cut the tension—before falling into a rhythm they hadn't used in decades but hadn't forgotten.

Jack gave a last scan of his crew—patched together, out of place in a world that had moved on, but sharp where it counted. Still his.

"Let's roll," he said.

By the time the lawn chairs filled out, the crew was already on the move. Billy steered the camper into the vendor lot like it belonged there—dusty, patched, and unnoticed. Behind him, Murphy's old Crown Vic rolled slow, carrying Jack, Murphy, and Sayers. Riley had gone ahead—press badge flashing, clipboard in hand, spinning believable lies about a misplaced flight manifest.

The small airport shimmered in the summer haze. Folding chairs bloomed across the grass like wildflowers. Kids with popsicles darted between veterans in campaign caps and families in flag shirts. Vendors hawked lemonade, fudge, and toy gliders beneath red and blue tents. A brass band tuned up by the makeshift grandstand.

From a riser near the announcer's booth, a local news station was already broadcasting. The camera panned across flags and polished wings. The on-screen graphic read: Wings of Freedom – LIVE from Harbor Springs!

A cheerful anchor in a cherry-red blazer leaned into the camera. "And just behind me, the final preparations are underway for today's spectacular Fourth of July flyover, featuring restored World War II aircraft and a few rumored surprises!"

Jack stood well beyond the crowd, arms crossed, eyes on the horizon.

His crew flanked him like ghosts of a formation long past: Murphy in mirrored aviators,

Sayers thumbing a wrench like a prayer bead, Billy bouncing on the balls of his feet. Riley, now in the field with other reporters, moved like she belonged —efficient, sharp, confident. Tommy stood nearby, camera bag slung over his shoulder like he was covering a war, not committing a caper.

They weren't watching the planes. They were watching time.

The real mission would begin in thirty minutes.

A rumble cut across the blacktop behind the maintenance shed.

The fuel truck rolled in slow—matte gray, unmarked, bearing Michigan farm plates. It pulled to a stop beside a shed marked Authorized Personnel Only. The driver stepped out, nodded once, and waited.

Murphy walked over without a word and handed off a folded envelope. Their handshake was quick, purposeful. The driver gave a half-salute, half-smirk, and climbed back into the cab.

"That's our gas," Murphy said as he returned. "She'll be full in fifteen. Enough to get us up, over, and out."

"Assuming she starts," Sayers muttered.

"She'll start," Jack said, with more conviction than question.

Just then, Riley stepped beside Murphy. Her tone was lower now, private.

"You good, Grandpa?" she asked without looking at him. "You feeling okay?"

Murphy patted his jacket pockets—one, then the other. "Got the nitro. Got the water. Got the gum."

"Gum?"

"Helps with the nerves," he said. Then, with a grin: "Not that I get nervous."

She smiled faintly. "You ever get nervous?"

"Only when it's worth it."

She gave his hand a brief squeeze. "Just checking. The old man's got backup now."

He gave a gruff nod, eyes softening. "Damn right I do."

Back on the tarmac, a man in a cowboy hat shouted about kettle corn over a bullhorn. The marching band passed the media van, tubas shining in the sun. One of the younger reporters flagged Riley down, mistaking her for network staff.

"You with the network?"

"Freelance," Riley said, not slowing. "But I'm the one you'll want on record when this thing goes sideways."

"Uh… maybe after the flyover?"

"Your loss."

Tucked behind ropes and sun-bleached canvas, she waited—half-hidden, fully unmistakable.

Jack knew the slope of that spine, the way her nose dipped just slightly left, like she was listening for orders.

The canvas couldn't hide it.

Peto's Key hadn't changed.

His breath caught—just a little.

He'd flown her across continents and over oceans. Trusted her when the sky turned black and the ground disappeared. Dropped cargo into jungle strips where the trees clawed at the fuselage and the air itself felt like fire.

Now, after all these years, she was still here.

Still standing. Still waiting. Their girl.

Nearby, a B-25's engines coughed and caught, drawing cheers from the crowd.

Billy leaned toward Jack. "You think they'll notice when we take her?"

Jack's eyes never left the canvas. "They'll notice when we're over the lake with the sun behind us. Until then, they'll be looking everywhere else."

Tommy squinted at the sky, then down at his watch. "Well, if we're going to steal a plane, might as well do it during peak applause."

He adjusted the strap on his camera bag. "Timing was always my specialty. Right behind poor decisions."

Riley consulted her clipboard, flipped a page. "Security rotation shifts in ten. That's our window."

Murphy cracked his knuckles. "Feels like the old days."

Jack shook his head. "No. This time, we choose the fight."

A breeze lifted the tarp just enough to catch the silver skin underneath. Dull, defiant. Ready.

Jack stepped forward, his fingers brushing the compass in his pocket.

"All right, boys and girl," he said. "It's almost go-time."

No speeches. No drama.

Just nods from a crew who knew what mattered.

This wasn't for headlines.

It was for memory.

For freedom.

For flight.

And somewhere between smoke and morning light, the past had come back for one last mission.

CHAPTER FIFTEEN
CLIMB ABOARD

The tarp peeled back like a secret finally told.

Slipping past security hadn't been easy—but it hadn't been impossible either.

Riley had timed everything to the second. Two guards were distracted at the vendor gate, locked in a funnel cake pricing dispute with a state senate hopeful. A third loitered near the tarmac gate, sipping coffee and pretending to watch the bandstand.

Then came the squirrel.

Soaked, tailless, and dragging a strand of parade bunting, it tore across the airfield like a rodent-shaped warhead. No one knew where it came from, possibly the dunk tank, possibly hell.

It shot through a table of model warbirds,

collided with the kettle corn stand, and launched itself into the Boy Scouts of Troop 238.

They'd been mid–flag drill rehearsal for the live TV feed. One scout screamed. Another dropped the Michigan flag and bolted. The bugler panicked and accidentally switched to "Taps."

The squirrel, wholly unfazed, backflipped into a tuba and vanished.

That was enough.

The guards abandoned their posts to join the chase—one shouting into a walkie-talkie, the other drawing a stun gun like he'd trained his whole life for this.

From behind a vendor tent, Riley tapped her earpiece.

"You're up. Five-minute window. Go."

She stood close enough to see, far enough not to interfere—as the crew moved. Deliberate. Quiet. Faster than they had any right to be.

Jack led with that unmistakable pilot's gait— every step more instinct than effort, like he was walking toward another jungle strip in the dark. Murphy followed slower, one hand inside his jacket. Riley felt a tightness in her chest. He hadn't told the others. Just her.

Sayers stuck close to Murphy's flank, scanning the tarmac like it was a combat zone. Billy flanked wide, sweeping the perimeter with a crooked grin that barely covered his nerves.

Tommy brought up the rear. He gave Riley a two-fingered salute.

"Guess I always wanted to go out doing something that made the papers."

Then he disappeared behind the signage.

From the riser near the announcer's booth, the Channel 7 camera crew panned the crowd. The emcee—a former weatherman in a star-spangled blazer—beamed into the mic.

"And now, folks, the moment we've all been waiting for—keep your eyes to the sky!"

But Riley wasn't watching the sky.

She was watching four men move toward a memory.

Sayers reached the C-47 first. He ducked beneath the ropes with the ease of someone who used to do this in the dark, under fire. He popped the hatch and dropped the ladder in one smooth motion.

Jack followed. Each rung creaked beneath his boots. His hand grazed the plane's warm sun-soaked and solid skin. Still holding.

Billy handed up a crate—headsets, maps, a rusted first-aid kit—before climbing in behind him.

Tommy paused just long enough to mutter, "If we're hijacking a vintage aircraft on live TV, I hope they spell our names right."

Then came Murphy.

From her vantage near the vendor tents, Riley saw him hesitate. Just a flicker. A pause at the ladder. His left hand hovered at his chest, then shifted to the rung.

A faint tremor ran through his fingers—small but telling.

He climbed slow but steady. Anyone else might've missed it. She didn't.

He hadn't told the others. Only her.

She folded her arms, clipboard swinging at her side, and kept her eyes on him until he disappeared into the belly of the aircraft.

No dramatics. No radio call. No interference.

Just a long, silent exhale.

She wouldn't stop him.

But she'd be ready if something went wrong.

She always was.

Inside the cockpit, Jack slid into the left seat like he'd never left it. The control column settled beneath his palm like a memory returning home. The leather cracked. The seat stiff. But everything was exactly where it belonged.

Sayers dropped into the engineer's chair and started flipping switches.

"Still runs on spit and faith," he muttered.

"More faith than spit these days," Billy said, securing the crate along the fuselage wall.

Tommy strapped in at the nav station, unfolding a map with the practiced snap of a man who'd once charted courses over mountains named on no map.

"Same rules as the Hump," he said softly. "Trust the numbers. Trust the compass. Trust her."

Murphy eased onto the bench just behind the cockpit bulkhead, near the old radio panel.

He exhaled slowly, wiping his brow. His color wasn't good. His breath caught short, but he masked it. Riley would've noticed, but Jack didn't. Jack was locked in now locked into the yoke, the engine hum, the mission.

"Let's light her up," Murphy said. His voice was steady. Like he had a headset on again.

Jack reached for the master switch.

"Copy that."

The starter whined. The propeller hesitated. Then—life.

The C-47 roared awake, coughing smoke and memory into the sky.

Outside, Riley backed into the vendor crowd just as the fireworks crew cracked a test volley—sharp, echoing blasts that turned every head toward the lake.

The fireworks drowned out the first sputter of engines—perfect cover.

She clicked her mic.

"Runway clear. You're a go."

In the cockpit, the dials trembled. Billy braced against the bulkhead.

"We're really doing this, huh?"

Tommy glanced up from his chart.

"Yup. History in the making. Or at least a hell of a headline."

Jack leaned forward. His fingers curled around the yoke.

"Engines sound good," he said.

"She's still got it," Sayers confirmed.

"She'd better," Murphy murmured. Then, under his breath—just for himself:

"No room for half-measures today."

Outside, no one noticed the C-47 begin to roll—slow, steady, deliberate—just another aircraft in the show.

It wasn't flashy.

But it was flying.

And inside the hum of hydraulics and throttle, the crew felt it—that old ache of purpose. Of flight. Of something bigger than memory. They remembered hauling crates out the cargo door over jungle clearings, praying the strip was long enough, praying the mountains would give them one more passage.

This wasn't about pageantry.

It was about goodbye.
Their girl.
Their sky.
Their mission.
And for one last time, the clock was running.

CHAPTER SIXTEEN
BORROWED WINGS

Twilight cast long shadows over the Harbor Springs runway as the old C-47 rolled into motion. She shuddered forward, engines coughing, then roaring awake like an echo from another time. Jack's hands were steady on the yoke, but his knuckles whitened. The old warbird rumbled, defiant and alive.

Inside the cockpit, the crew locked into roles that muscle memory hadn't forgotten. Tommy, navigator once more, called out speeds. Billy, their de facto engineer, scanned gauges with a grease-blackened finger. Sayers, crew chief and mechanic, crouched at the bulkhead, listening with his ear more than his instruments. Murphy, the loadmaster, sat behind them—breathing shallow, one hand pressed to his chest, trying to mask the ache that had become harder to ignore.

"Pressure's steady," Billy called.

"Copy that," Jack said. "Here we go, boys."

The tail lifted. The wings caught wind. The C-47 was airborne.

Below, chaos bloomed. Airshow coordinators spilled from the hangar, shouting into walkie-talkies. Riley, flanked by stunned volunteers, marched toward the nearest camera crew.

"This isn't a theft," she said, her voice shaking but strong. "It's a reunion. A tribute. That plane—Peto's Key—flew over the Himalayas in 1944. Those men up there? They hauled wounded soldiers, rations, fuel—through storms that swallowed mountains, through enemy fire over jungle strips where there was no margin for error. They didn't just fly cargo. They carried hope."

She looked skyward, eyes fierce.

"My grandfather was just a boy then. Now he's an old man with a failing heart. But he didn't want to fade away in a hospital bed. He wanted to fly. Just one more time."

Her voice cracked. She steadied it.

"And he's not the only one. Every man on that plane lost something they never got back—brothers, years, pieces of themselves. They weren't looking for glory. They just did what was asked. And now, for once, we see them not as fading names in a book, but as living proof of courage, of memory, of love."

The reporter, stunned, passed her the mic. "And you are?"

"Riley Shaw. Granddaughter of Frank Murphy—loadmaster. Veteran. Heart patient." She swallowed. "He wanted to go out flying, not fading."

Crowds stilled. Heads tilted upward.

In the cockpit, Jack leveled off, the lake sparkling beneath.

"Gear up," he said. Tommy complied.

"You see that tower losing their minds?" Billy muttered with a grin.

"I see 'em," Jack replied. "Tower is on one. Let's hear it."

Static crackled, then a sharp voice:

"Unidentified C-47, this is Harbor Springs Control. You are not cleared for departure. State your intentions immediately."

Jack toggled the mic. "Captain Jack Whitaker, United States Army Air Corps. Retired—but not grounded. Crew aboard. Requesting a ceremonial flyover. Non-hostile. Just nostalgic."

"Unidentified C-47, divert immediately or face interception."

"Guess they noticed," Billy muttered.

Tommy smirked. "Tell 'em we're too old to dogfight, but we'll still outfly their rulebook."

Jack's eyes flicked to the horizon. "Let's hope Riley buys us time."

On the ground, she was doing exactly that. News crews swiveled. Announcers scrambled. Veterans in campaign caps saluted with trembling hands. A kid in a Top Gun T-shirt pointed skyward.

And tucked in Riley's bag, a folded photo of Sarah—Jack's wife, smiling from another lifetime—waited like a secret witness. Riley whispered toward the horizon: "He's doing it, Sarah. Just like you knew he would."

High above, Murphy shifted in his seat. His lips were pale. His hand trembled on the frame.

"Frank?" Jack called back. "You with us?"

Murphy opened one eye. "I'm fine. Just

taking in the view." His voice was thin. A beat later, he added, almost to himself: "Feels like the Hump again. Just colder inside."

Tommy caught Billy's look. Neither spoke.

The C-47 banked over the bay, twilight catching her worn silver skin. Along the nose, a faded scar of paint hinted at her old name, known only to those inside.

At Coast Guard Air Station Traverse City, two HH-65 Dolphins stood fueled. A junior officer asked, "Commander, are we really scrambling on a vintage warbird?"

"Not yet," came the reply. "If they head for the bridge, then we intervene."

Back in the cockpit, static returned.

"Unidentified C-47, you are not authorized for flyover."

Jack exhaled. "We'll be quick. Just a pass."

Billy ran his checks. "Throttle's holding. She's stronger than we are."

Murphy chuckled weakly. "Speak for yourself. I feel ninety."

Jack smiled faintly. "And still hauling freight."

The words hung—a callback not just to missions past, but to the bond that made them more than survivors.

Below, the crowd swelled into applause. A father lifted his daughter and whispered, "That's not a museum plane. That's history." Veterans stood at attention. A little girl raised her sparkler like a torch. Pride swept the field.

Jack's voice went quiet. "Boys… this one's for every crew that didn't make it home."

Tommy laid a hand on his shoulder. "Let's make it count."

They turned toward Little Traverse Bay, toward Petoskey. Below, families poured from porches and rooftops, eyes lifted to the fading silver bird.

It wasn't theft anymore. It was a homecoming. A salute. A final loop through time—by the hands of the men who once flew her through fire and storm, and who now carried her back to where she belonged.

Riley stepped from the news van, shielding her eyes, whispering into the glow of the bay:

"Fly her all the way home."

And above, framed by twilight and lake water, Peto's Key climbed into memory—borrowed wings bearing one last mission.

CHAPTER SEVENTEEN
THE SKY BELONGS TO THEM

The C-47 leveled off after the pass over Petoskey, engines drumming steady against the summer air. From the cockpit, Little Traverse Bay spread out like glass, dotted with sailboats and fishing craft. Jack eased the yoke, eyes scanning the horizon.

"Beautiful, isn't she?" Tommy said, nodding toward the shoreline below.

"Always was," Jack replied. "Even in winter."

Billy, still watching the gauges, glanced over his shoulder. "Frank, how're we doing?"

Murphy sat slumped against the bulkhead, his breathing thin. He gave a crooked smile. "Don't count me out yet." But his hand never left his chest.

Sayers shifted closer, eyes flicking between Murphy and the instruments. "Don't push him, Captain. The engines can take strain — he can't."

Jack didn't like the look of him. "We keep her steady. No hero turns."

Tommy grinned faintly. "Too late for that, Captain. We're already in the middle of one."

Down on the ground, Riley stood near the museum's staging tent, her hair windblown from the passing propwash. The crowd had surged since takeoff—more reporters, more cameras, more people drawn in by the sound of the engines overhead.

Two men in plain jackets pushed their way through, flashing ID.

"Miss Shaw," the taller one said evenly, "we'd like a word about your involvement."

Riley crossed her arms. "You can have one. In front of them." She gestured to the TV cameras now pivoting in her direction.

The shorter man hesitated. "Ma'am, this is an active federal matter—"

"It's a matter of respect," Riley cut in, her voice rising, meant for the lenses more than the agents. "Those men up there aren't fugitives. They're veterans. And that plane? She isn't a museum relic — she's the reason some of them lived to come home. My grandfather is one of them, and he's dying. That cockpit is the only place he still knows who he is. They flew through storms over the Himalayas when the world needed them — and you'd stop them here, over their own hometown? Take that away, and you're not protecting history — you're erasing it."

A murmur rippled through the onlookers. Someone clapped—then another—and soon a small wave of applause grew into cheers. Several veterans removed their caps and stood at attention.

One old paratrooper near the front cupped his hands to his mouth: "Let 'em fly! They crossed the Hump — they can cross this bay!"

The crowd roared in answer, picking up the chant: "Let them fly! Let them fly!" Microphones swung closer. The agents backed off, realizing the moment was slipping from their hands.

From the Bayfront Park seawall, kids waved flags and pointed upward. A portable AM radio, propped on a cooler, crackled with a live broadcast: "Unidentified vintage warbird now banking south along the shoreline… crowd reaction here is nothing short of electric…"

On rooftops downtown, families leaned over railings to catch a glimpse. Out on the water, boaters laid on their horns in salute. A fisherman in a small skiff lifted his cap and held it over his heart.

A boater's voice came over a CB channel: "Breaker one-nine, you seeing this old girl? She's low and she's moving south. Like the old days."

At the Coast Guard Air Station in Traverse City, a junior officer stepped into the CO's office, holding a ringing phone. "Sir, that's the tenth one in five minutes. They're all calling to say don't stop them."

The CO leaned back, eyes on the radar screen. "Then maybe we wait. Let the sky have them a little longer."

In the cockpit, the air was warm and smelled faintly of oil and canvas.

"Remember that run to Kunming?" Tommy said, smiling at the memory. "Storm so bad we couldn't see the wingtip."

Murphy chuckled weakly. "Jack still landed smoother than most fellas on a sunny day."

Sayers gave a faint laugh. "Engines were coughing fire the whole way. Talked 'em through every mile like they were scared kids. Guess they believed me."

Billy grinned, but his eyes stayed on Murphy. "You sure you're good back there?"

Murphy's answer came quiet, but steady. "Reckon we've got one more pass in us?"

Sayers leaned forward from his seat, hand resting on the bulkhead as if steadying the whole airframe. "Engines will hold. She wants this as much as we do."

Jack looked back at him, then at Tommy.

Tommy gave a small nod. "Be a shame not to, with the light just right."

Jack smiled faintly. "Alright, Frank. One more sweep."

He eased the yoke, and the C-47 banked wide, wings glinting in the last gold wash of the setting sun. Below, the bay mirrored streaks of crimson and orange, dotted with sailboats and fireworks barges preparing for the night show.

The crowd on the shoreline erupted as the old bird roared past again—flags waving, voices carrying faintly up to the cockpit.

Murphy closed his eyes, letting the sound and vibration of the engines fill the silence. "Now that's the way to remember it," he murmured.

Sayers kept his gaze fixed on the gauges, nodding once. "She's singing tonight, Frank. Just like she used to."

Onshore, Riley shaded her eyes against the sun, watching the silver shape turn above the bay.

"They're not done yet," she told the nearest reporter. "Not by a long shot."

Above, the C-47 droned on, wings flashing in the last light — carrying her crew into one final sweep of sky, refusing to land.

CHAPTER EIGHTEEN
THE LONG WAY DOWN

The engines held steady, the rhythmic growl vibrating through the cockpit floor. A faint tang of oil and hot metal hung in the warm cabin air, mixing with the sharp scent of canvas and dust that had been part of the old bird for decades. Jack kept his eyes on the shoreline, where twilight painted the water in ribbons of fire and rose.

"We're burning daylight," Billy said quietly, eyes flicking between gauges.

Tommy checked the fuel. "And fuel."

Jack nodded. "We'll bring her in soon." But his voice carried no urgency, just a stubborn reluctance to let the moment end.

Behind them, Murphy shifted and winced, his boots scraping softly against the deck. Jack caught it in the side mirror and frowned. "Frank, talk to me."

"Just air's a little thin up here," Murphy said. "I'm fine." But his hand still pressed against his ribs, and his breathing stayed shallow.

Below, the shoreline pulsed with life—a living ripple of flags and flashes. Cheers and whistles merged with the crackle of radios as sound spilled into the streets, stretching from the airport grounds to the Bayfront Park seawall. Porch lights flicked on block by block, neighbors spilling out with folding chairs and coolers. From rooftops and balconies, families leaned out with flags and sparklers. A fire truck on State Street gave a proud, echoing blast of its horn, answered by car horns all the way to the waterfront. It was as if the entire town had tipped onto its feet to salute the sky.

A diner on State Street had rolled its TV into the doorway; people leaned in through the windows to watch grainy footage, the live anchor's voice breaking now and then under the noise from outside.

"They're coming back around," the anchor

announced, the words barely audible over the roar of the crowd outside the diner.

Riley stood on the seawall, answering reporters' questions with a conviction that grew stronger each time she spoke. The agents lingered nearby but didn't interrupt; she'd won the crowd, and they knew it.

One reporter leaned in with a question: "What happens when they land?"

Riley smiled faintly, eyes never leaving the sky. "That's their call. But no matter what happens next… the sky belongs to them tonight."

Another microphone appeared in front of her. "Miss Shaw—how's your grandfather holding up?"

Riley took a breath, her voice catching just slightly. "He's tired. He's been through more than anyone should have to. But right now... he's exactly where he belongs. And that means everything to him."

"And the rest of the crew?" someone shouted from the back.

Her smile grew. "They're brothers. They've been brothers since the Hump. I think some part of them never left that cockpit. Tonight, you're all seeing who they've been all along."

The murmurs grew into clapping, then cheers. Microphones swung closer. The agents backed off another step, the crowd closing in to shield her like she was one of their own.

In the cockpit, Tommy tapped the fuel gauge. "We can squeeze maybe fifteen more minutes if we keep her steady."

Sayers leaned forward, listening as if the engines were whispering to him. "She's still got a little left in her. Let her sing."

"That's all I need," Jack said.

Murphy's voice drifted forward, weaker now. "Jack… reckon we've got one more pass in us?"

Jack glanced at Tommy, who gave a small nod. "One more," Jack said.

The C-47 banked wide, her wings slicing through the last gold wash of the setting sun. The bay below caught every streak of color—deep crimson where the fireworks barges sat waiting, silver where the water lay still.

From the shoreline came a swell of cheering

that punched through the engine noise. Down in the park, a little boy climbed onto his father's shoulders, waving a sparkler that traced bright loops against the darkening sky. Two elderly veterans stood side by side, hats pressed to their chests, eyes glistening.

Billy grinned. "Listen to that. Sounds like 1945 down there."

Tommy nodded. "Feels like V-E Day — for a few more minutes."

And below, the ripple spread again—flags flaring, porch lights glowing, horns blasting up and down the shoreline. Fireworks crews on the barges stopped their work to wave. Kids sprinted barefoot across the grass to keep pace with the shadow overhead. On Main Street, people spilled out of shops and bars, drawn by the roar, every face turned skyward. The whole town seemed to lift with the plane, riding its echo through the evening air.

At the Coast Guard station, the CO stood at the radio console, headset resting around his neck. "Still holding south of the bridge," an operator reported.

The CO studied the radar, then shook his head. "No intercept. Let them have their finish."

Riley's eyes followed the plane until it faded against the darkening sky. Around her, strangers were hugging, veterans were saluting, and kids were shouting for the pilots to keep flying. The shoreline felt like it had tipped into another time— one where rules didn't matter as much as respect.

She turned back toward the cameras. "If you're watching this from home, step outside. Look up. They're writing their story in the sky tonight."

Back in the cockpit, Jack leveled off and took a long breath. "Alright, boys. Let's take her home."

Murphy gave a slow smile. "Best Fourth since the war. Haven't heard engines sing like this since Kunming."

Tommy reached back and squeezed his shoulder. "We're not done yet, Frank."

Jack set a gentle course toward the airfield, the runway lights beginning to wink on through the dusk. The engines kept their steady song — a sound Sayers had spent his life listening to, and one none of them ever wanted to forget.

CHAPTER NINETEEN
HOME ON THE GROUND

The C-47 touched down with a chirp of tires and a low, rolling rumble. Jack held her steady down the centerline, letting her speed bleed off before easing onto the brakes. The crowd beyond the fence was impossible to miss—an unbroken line of people pressed shoulder to shoulder, spilling down the taxiway edge.

Billy leaned toward the side window. "Never thought I'd see this many folks waiting for us without MPs in the mix."

Tommy smirked. "Yeah, well… if they cuff us, at least we'll go out to a standing ovation."

Jack guided the old bird toward the main apron on the far side of the terminal. The propellers spun down slowly, the deep, rhythmic growl fading into the gentle tick of cooling metal. He killed the switches one by one, each click echoing in the cabin.

For a moment, no one moved. The quiet felt heavy after hours of vibration and engine noise.

Murphy broke it with a rasp of a chuckle. "Don't just sit there, boys. We made it."

On the tarmac, the wall of people shifted closer. Veterans in faded caps stood at the front, some saluting, some simply watching with damp eyes. Behind them, news crews jostled for position. The crowd noise swelled, voices calling out names, cheering, clapping.

Riley was there—exactly where she had been for the last few passes—by the rope line near the main terminal gate. She'd planted herself at the best vantage point for the landing and hadn't moved since. The agents were still a few steps behind her, silent now, almost blending into the background.

Jack opened the side window and raised a hand. The cheer that came back rolled over the apron in a rush.

Murphy lifted his hand in a smaller wave. Riley felt her throat tighten.

Sayers appeared in the hatchway for a moment, one hand resting on the frame as though steadying the old bird herself. He gave a short nod toward the crowd, then turned back inside to help guide Murphy.

Jack appeared at the door behind him, one hand gripping the frame. "We'll need a couple minutes to get him down careful," he said to no one in particular, but his eyes stayed on Riley.

She nodded, pressing her palm to her chest. "Take your time."

The crowd, still pressed in around the apron, had gone quieter—cheers fading into hushed murmurs, the kind that fall over a congregation when reverence takes hold. The engines ticked as they cooled, the scent of hot oil drifting across the summer night air.

Tommy came to the door next, leaning out to scan the sea of faces. Families stood shoulder to shoulder, veterans misty-eyed, kids on parents' shoulders waving tiny flags like torchbearers. "Never thought we'd draw this kind of homecoming," he muttered. "Back then, we just stepped off a transport and caught the next train. No bands, no flags. Just silence."

"You earned it," someone shouted from the crowd, and a ripple of agreement moved through the onlookers.

Ground crew rolled a short stair set to the cargo door. Jack and Billy eased Murphy to his feet, each taking an arm. Riley stepped forward instinctively but stopped just short of the safety rope. She wanted to run to him, to close the distance, but she also knew these few steps down were his to take.

Murphy's boots touched the tarmac with a hollow thud, a sound that carried farther than it should have. The crowd erupted again—not wild, but warm. Sustained applause, clapping in rhythm, veterans raising their caps in salute.

Riley crossed to him at last. Up close, she could see how pale he was, how every breath seemed an effort. But when she reached for his hand, his grip was still strong.

"You did it," she whispered.

His smile deepened, lines creasing around his eyes. "We did it."

Jack stepped down behind them, his gaze sweeping the crowd, then the horizon where the last traces of twilight clung above the bay. "Let's get him inside," he said quietly, but there was pride in his voice.

As they moved across the apron, ground handlers guided them toward the operations hangar—far from any exhibit space but well-lit and accessible. Camera flashes strobed across the tarmac. Somewhere behind them, the announcer's voice carried over a loudspeaker: "Ladies and gentlemen, the crew of the C-47 that just made history tonight."

The words followed them into the shadows of the hangar, where the night seemed to hold its breath—waiting for whatever came next. And above it all, the engines ticked as they cooled — a sound Sayers listened to like a doctor hearing the last steady beat of a heart he'd tended all his life.

CHAPTER TWENTY
A PLACE TO LAND

The hangar doors stood half-open, the last threads of twilight spilling across the concrete floor. Inside, the air was cooler, still carrying the tang of oil, dust, and old paint. The C-47 loomed just outside, her silver skin catching the glow of portable floodlights being rolled into place.

Murphy lowered himself onto a folding chair someone had pulled from the corner. His breathing was slow, measured, his eyes closed for a moment as though memorizing the feel of the cool metal seat beneath him. Riley crouched beside him, one hand resting on his knee.

"Medics are coming," she said softly. "They're just outside."

He shook his head faintly. "Let 'em take their time. Feels good to just sit in the quiet."

Jack stood a few paces away, Tommy and Billy beside him. They hadn't taken their eyes off Murphy since they got him down the stairs. Sayers had dragged the folding chair over himself, then lingered a moment with his palm pressed against the fuselage, like a mechanic listening for echoes in the steel. Only then did he step back toward Murphy, his usual quiet wrapped in relief.

From the hangar opening, a murmur of voices swelled—the sound of the crowd being held back just beyond the rope lines. Then came the sharper, more deliberate footsteps of the officials moving in. Two EMTs appeared first, carrying a small kit and a folded stretcher. Behind them, the agents who had shadowed Riley all afternoon stepped into the light, their expressions unreadable.

One of the EMTs knelt in front of Murphy. "Sir, we just want to check your vitals, alright?"

Murphy opened his eyes and gave a dry chuckle. "You can check whatever you like, long as you don't tell me I can't fly anymore."

The medic smiled faintly and began working.

The agents glanced toward Riley, but she met their gaze without flinching. "You're not laying a hand on him," she said. "Not tonight."

"We're not here for that," the taller agent replied, voice low enough that only she and the crew could hear. "There'll be conversations later. For now… the crowd's made it pretty clear what they think."

Outside, the cheering hadn't stopped—it was a steady, rhythmic applause that carried into the hangar like a heartbeat.

One of the EMTs looked up from his kit. "He's stable, but we need to get him somewhere with oxygen."

Murphy waved a hand. "Not yet. Just… give me a minute with my crew."

The medics hesitated, then stepped back.

Jack crossed the floor and rested a hand on Murphy's shoulder. "You alright to stand for a picture?"

Murphy's smile returned. "Hell yes."

Tommy laughed and clapped him lightly on the back. "One for the books."

Billy moved toward the door, calling to the nearest photographer. "Get over here—these boys aren't going anywhere until you get this shot."

The flashbulbs popped in quick succession, freezing the moment in white light: four men who had once crossed the sky together in war, reunited in peace for one final flight. Sayers didn't smile for the cameras so much as tip his head toward the old bird outside, making sure she was caught in the frame too. Four men, and the plane that had bound them together.

Riley stayed just behind them, tears stinging her eyes, knowing the photo would outlast the night, the summer, maybe even their names.

When the cameras finally dropped, Murphy leaned toward her. "Alright, kid. Now you can let the medics fuss."

She laughed through the lump in her throat. "Deal."

As they guided him to a cot near the rear wall of the hangar, propped up slightly with folded blankets, the crowd outside broke into cheers again, this time chanting a single phrase that rolled over the night air like a promise—

"The sky belongs to them! The sky belongs to them!"

The chant faded slowly, but its echo seemed to settle into the steel beams above them, into the bones of the hangar itself.

A Coast Guard officer stepped quietly into the hangar, pausing at the edge of the group. He was young, respectful, and clearly aware of the gravity of the moment.

"Captain Whitaker? Sir, I just wanted to say… what you all did tonight—no one will forget it. We monitored it from the tower. It was... inspiring."

Jack nodded. "Appreciate that, son."

Tommy and Billy sat off to the side on an old bench, sipping coffee from Styrofoam cups passed around by one of the airport staff. They were quiet, their energy spent but their expressions light. The kind of peace that only comes after finishing something impossible.

"Think we're going to get a medal for this?" Billy asked after a pause.

"Nah," Tommy said, lifting his cup. "But I'll take the coffee."

A laugh passed between them. The mood had shifted—not celebration, exactly, but something close to contentment.

Outside the hangar, the crowd hadn't thinned—in fact, it had grown. Word had spread across town. Families came from porches and parks, drawn by the sound of engines and the sight of history made real. Many pressed close to the rope lines and fences, hoping for a glimpse, a handshake, or simply to share in something they'd tell their grandkids about someday.

Inside, Riley leaned close to Murphy. "You comfortable?"

"I'm fine, sweetheart," he rasped. "Just tired. Not from flying. From holding all this in for so many years."

Her eyes shimmered.

Murphy smiled. "I got to fly with my brothers. Got to hear the engines again. Got to feel weightless... just once more. That's everything."

Riley squeezed his hand. "You let it out tonight. The whole town saw. And they'll never forget it."

Murphy nodded slowly, his hand still curled

around hers. A silence fell between them—thick with years, lifted by what they had just done.

A teenage voice piped up from the hangar entrance. "Mr. Murphy?"

They turned to see the young reporter from earlier—the one with the big notepad and wide eyes. He was now holding a small handheld tape recorder and wearing a Petoskey High School Highlighter badge clipped to his jacket.

The Coast Guard officer looked about to intervene, but Riley waved him off.

"Give him a shot," she said softly. "He's earned it."

The kid approached carefully. "Sir, I—I mean, Mr. Murphy... would you be willing to say a few words? Just for the school paper. Everyone's still watching out there."

Murphy raised a brow, then nodded faintly. "Sure, kid. Roll tape."

The teen crouched beside him, tape recorder up.

"Frank Murphy, Loadmaster of the C-47 that flew tonight's tribute—what do you want people to remember?"

Murphy licked his lips and spoke slowly. "I want them to remember... that freedom didn't come cheap. That some of us carried more than supplies—we carried each other. And tonight... we carried a memory back into the sky."

The hangar went quiet again.

Jack turned away, eyes misted. Billy stared into his coffee. Tommy let out a low whistle. Sayers finally exhaled, rubbing a hand across his jaw. "Couldn't have said it better," he muttered, the kind of praise that carried more weight than a headline.

Murphy leaned back and closed his eyes. "Now... I could use a damn nap."

Laughter followed. Gentle. Honest.

A place to land.

CHAPTER TWENTY-ONE
THE QUIET AFTER

The hangar had thinned to a hush. Floodlights hummed, cameras clicked half-heartedly, and the crowd outside had settled into a distant murmur that came and went with the breeze.

Murphy dozed lightly on the cot, Riley still at his side. His chest rose and fell slow, steady. A medic sat a few feet away, clipboard balanced on his knee, close enough to act, far enough to give them the moment.

Jack leaned against a support beam, arms crossed, eyes on the silver fuselage parked just beyond the open doors. For a long while he said nothing. Then, quietly:

"She's flown her last flight."

Sayers looked up from the wheel well, rag

blackened with grease in his hand. "If a plane could be tired, she'd be it. But hell, she gave us more than we had any right to ask."

Billy whistled low. "Feels strange. Spent half my life climbing into something like her. Now I don't know what to do with both feet on the ground."

Tommy, perched on an overturned toolbox, tilted his head. "Maybe that's the point. We did what we came to do. Gave her a sendoff—gave ourselves one, too."

The words settled over them. Nobody rushed to fill the quiet.

Outside, late fireworks popped over the bay—soft, far-off—casting brief, shifting patterns along the hangar wall.

Riley stood, smoothing a hand over her face. Her voice was clear, though her throat was tight. "You all gave this town something they'll never forget. Doesn't matter what the headlines say tomorrow. Tonight… it was yours."

Murphy stirred, opened one eye. "Ours? Nah." His voice was a rasp, but steady. "Belongs to every kid who looked up and figured we still had it in us."

From the open doors, a lone voice started "God Bless America," cracked but true. Others joined. The words drifted in like smoke, like prayer. Jack's lips moved with the chorus; the sound caught in his throat.

When the song faded, a good quiet returned.

That was when the agents stepped out of the shadows. They hadn't spoken in hours. The taller one cleared his throat, tone measured. "There'll be questions in the morning. Statements. Some procedural things—airspace, custody of the aircraft."

Billy rolled his eyes. Jack didn't move. Riley did.

"Tomorrow," she said, and the word had weight. "Not tonight. The people outside made their choice. You want statements, you'll get them after sunup."

The shorter agent glanced toward the doors, listened to the murmur beyond, and gave a small nod. "Understood. No arrests tonight. The aircraft stays put under a soft hold. We'll coordinate with the museum and the airport."

A figure in a polo with an airport badge and another with a museum lanyard had drifted closer, drawn by the exchange. Riley turned to them.

"She doesn't get shoved in a dark corner after this," Riley said. "Tomorrow, doors open. People can come see her, tell their stories. After that, we'll talk about where she belongs—somewhere alive. Not behind velvet ropes."

The museum rep hesitated, then looked out toward the crowd and back again. "We can do a public viewing day," she said. "Document everything, gather names, photos. Let the town help us prove what she is."

Sayers's mouth tipped in the barest smile. "She'll like the company."

A medic leaned in toward Murphy, checking a pulse oximeter, his voice low. "Sir, your oxygen's slipping. We can keep you stable here for a few minutes, but we should transport soon."

Murphy breathed out through his nose, a wry almost-laugh. "Always with the schedule."

Jack moved to the cot, the command in him softened by age. "Frank, let them do their job. We'll ride point on the debrief in the morning."

Murphy eyed him, then Riley. "I'll go if she comes."

Riley nodded at once. "I'm with you."

Sayers reached into a canvas toolbox and produced a small green bottle, patched and scuffed. "Portable O_2 from the bird. She carried us; she can carry him a little farther." He fitted the cannula with the ease of a man who'd done a hundred field fixes. The medic checked the gauge, gave an approving grunt, and clipped a monitor to Murphy's finger.

Tommy stood, thumbed a sweat-creased cap, and placed it in Murphy's hands. "You'll want this."

"Damn right I will," Murphy said, and for a heartbeat he looked twenty years younger.

Billy stepped toward the agents, lowering his voice. "And us?"

"0900," the taller one said. "Statements in the conference room. Nobody leaves town. Paperwork, not cuffs."

Billy tipped an invisible hat. "Paperwork I can live with."

The Coast Guard CO appeared in the doorway, soft-spoken as before. "We'll clear a path to the hospital. Lights, no sirens. Folks will make room."

Outside, the crowd began to ebb—families shepherding tired kids to cars, veterans lingering at the rope to stare a little longer. The chant was gone now, replaced by the shuffle and murmur of a town returning to itself.

Inside, the crew gathered close without being asked. Jack at Murphy's shoulder, Tommy and Billy flanking, Sayers a step behind with the green bottle steady in his fist. Riley walked alongside, fingers threaded with Murphy's.

They moved together toward the doors, into the wash of cooler night air. The portable floodlights threw long shadows across the concrete, five silhouettes and a sixth looming just beyond—the old bird itself, still and silver.

At the threshold, Murphy paused and looked back at her. "Good girl," he said, barely above a whisper.

Sayers's knuckles grazed the fuselage one last time, a mechanic's benediction. "We'll see you in the morning."

Reporters parted without questions. The agents stood aside. The town made a lane.

"Alright, boys," Jack said, the words quiet and familiar. "Debrief at 0900. Until then—"

"—get some rack time," Tommy finished, grinning despite himself.

Billy chuckled. "After all this, I might actually sleep."

They eased Murphy into the ambulance. Riley climbed in after him. The CO raised two fingers in a small salute; Jack returned it.

The doors thudded shut. The engine turned over. The vehicle rolled forward, slow and respectful, taillights glowing red against the dark.

Back in the hangar, the floodlights hummed. The plane waited, dignified and still.

Tomorrow would ask for statements and signatures. Tonight had already given them what papers never could.

CHAPTER TWENTY-TWO
THE LAST WATCH

Dawn crept in pale and quiet, filtering through the blinds of the hospital room. Machines hummed, wheels rolled faintly on linoleum, but inside the room the world felt hushed, waiting.

Murphy rested in the cot, oxygen hissing low beside him. His chest rose and fell in stubborn, steady rhythm. Riley sat at his side, her hand folded over his, her gaze shifting toward the window where the first commuter flights painted contrails above the bay. She hadn't slept, but she wasn't tired in a way that mattered.

Jack stepped in, hat in hand, boots too heavy for the hush. He lingered in the doorway before crossing to the bed.

"He's got more fight in him than any of us ever did," he said quietly.

Riley smiled faintly, though her eyes shimmered. "He carried the war his whole life. Last night, it carried him home."

Jack's gaze dropped to the nightstand. Half-hidden under a clipboard lay a creased photograph of Sarah—his Sarah. Someone had taken it from the cockpit and set it there, like a benediction. His hand hesitated, then picked it up. The smile he had carried through a thousand miles of jungle stared back. For years it had been a wound. Now it felt like something else—something he could keep without bleeding.

He slipped the photo carefully into his breast pocket.

"She came along for the ride," he murmured. "Guess she knew how much I needed it."

Later that morning, the hangar doors rolled wide to let sunlight flood in. The C-47 gleamed silver under the glow, as if warmed back to life.

The crew was there—Jack, Tommy, Billy, Sayers—watching as townspeople streamed in.

Veterans pressed hands to the fuselage. Families lifted children to touch the rivets. Camera flashes sparked. It wasn't noise. It was testimony.

Riley laid her hand against the nose. "Not just an exhibit," she said, her voice carrying. "She belongs to all of you now. She belongs alive."

Her words rippled outward, agreement murmured in pockets of the crowd.

Sayers, crouched by the wheel well with a rag in his hand, managed a thin smile. "She'll like the company."

Billy whistled low. "Whole damn town showed up."

Tommy nodded, duffel slung off his shoulder. "Guess we weren't the only ones who needed to see her fly again." He pulled out his old baseball glove—the same one that had followed him from Burma to bingo halls—and eased it into the pilot's seat through the open hatch. "Carried me through plenty of nights. Now it can stay with her."

The glove slumped into place like it belonged.

Jack followed, drawing Sarah's photo from his pocket. His thumb brushed her face once before he set it on the dash beside the glove. Memory and promise. Love and play. Two relics, stitched into the bird's last resting place.

For a moment he lingered, lips moving in a whisper meant for her alone.

"I'm still here, Sarah. Still flying. But I'll land, too."

The crew stood together in the hangar's glow while the town claimed the story as its own. The plane had flown her last flight, but the memory had only just landed.

EPILOGUE
ONE MORE TABLE

Three days later, the diner smelled of bacon grease and burnt coffee. The booth by the window sagged, but it fit them: Jack, Tommy, Billy, Sayers, and Riley.

Murphy couldn't be there—still in the hospital, steady but resting—but his absence didn't leave silence. It left presence, woven into the laughter and the steam curling off their mugs.

Billy poked at his pie. "Think they'll pin a medal on us?"

Tommy snorted into his coffee. "Nah. Paperwork, maybe. Coffee if we're lucky."

Sayers wiped his hands on a napkin. "I'll take sleep over medals."

They laughed—the kind of laugh that only

comes when the danger is past and the weight has been shared.

Riley leaned back, watching them, smiling. She didn't feel like an outsider anymore. She felt woven into their story.

Jack raised his mug. "To the bird."

Tommy lifted his cup. "To the crew."

Billy clinked his glass. "To the kid who kept us honest."

Sayers added, "And to tomorrow."

Riley raised hers last, voice soft but sure. "To Peto's Key."

The cups touched. Outside, a commuter jet droned overhead, unnoticed—just another sound in a sky once crossed by bigger storms.

Jack in the hangar by the bay, the glove still rested in the cockpit, the photograph propped beside it. Memory and presence, side by side.

And in Jack's pocket, another photograph waited—creased, worn, carried forward this time not as a wound but as a companion. His fingers brushed it once, like a man who finally knew that home could live both in the sky and on the ground.

The story had found its place to land.

THE FINAL ORDERS

Typed not for war, but for memory. Not for a
supply line, but for a circle flown over waters
that once seemed impossibly far away.

CONFIDENTIAL
> Remembrance Flight – Independent Veter-
> ans Group
> Little Traverse Bay, Northern Michigan

HEADQUARTERS
> Independent Veterans Association
> Petoskey, Michigan
> 4 July 1985

MISSION SUMMARY – REMEMBRANCE
FLIGHT
> MISSION NO. 1 – Commemorative flight

around Little Traverse Bay, honoring veterans of Hump operations, 1327th AAF Base Unit.

AIRCRAFT
    a. Type: Douglas C-47 Skytrain (restored)
    b. Tail No.: [REDACTED]
    c. Call Sign: Dogtail Four (honorary)

CREW
    Capt. J. Whitaker (Ret.)
    Lt. T. Murphy (Ret.) [present in spirit; hospitalized, unable to attend]
    T/Sgt. A. LeClair (Ret.)
    T/Sgt. H. Sayers (Ret.)
    Cpl. T. Dillard (Ret.)

CARGO
None, save memory carried aloft.

RESULTS
Aircraft departed Harbor Springs Airfield 0930 hrs. Completed ceremonial circuit over Little Traverse Bay, circling Petoskey, Bay View,

and Harbor Springs. Landing 1015 hrs without incident. Shoreline crowds recorded attendance.

COMMENTS

Flight conducted in remembrance of WWII service, Hump operations 1943–1945. Symbolic completion of missions once begun in Assam, Burma, and China. Endurance of crew testimony affirms both sacrifice and survival.

FILED BY:

Independent Veterans Association
Commemorative Committee

The report ended in type and ink, but what it could not say was the way the bay shone beneath the wings, or how the sound of the engines carried across the water like a remembered hymn. It did not note the faces turned skyward, or the silence that fell when the circle was complete. The document closed with a date and a stamp, but the true record was written in the air itself—where duty became memory, and memory, at last, became home.

www.ingramcontent.com/pod-product-compliance
Lightning Source LLC
Chambersburg PA
CBHW020803310726
48969CB00002B/680